ADVENTURES WITH Hugo

A lighter look at the dark side of addiction

David Anton

ISBN (paperback) - 978-1-9164589-0-1
ISBN (epub) - 978-1-9164589-1-8
ISBN (mobi) - 978-1-9164589-2-5

Printed in the United Kingdom

Cover design and layout by www.spiffingcovers.com

About the Author

Dr David Anton is a retired physician with a lifelong interest in how things go wrong and how people are affected by the consequences. He spent half his medical career in the Royal Air Force investigating aircraft accidents, before moving to civilian life where he specialised in the interactions of health with work. This is his first foray into writing a humorous novel with serious intent. He has owned two springer spaniels and two Labradors, breeds as joyous and as incorrigible as you could find.

Acknowledgements

This book arose out of a chance encounter with a hopelessly food-addicted Labrador. Hugo really exists, as does his owner, to whom I owe a debt of gratitude that can never be repaid. W. Sitch & Co used to be near the top of Berwick Street in Soho, London, but sadly closed during the writing of this book. The Sitch brothers, who were at least the thirteenth generation of the family in their business, kindly gave their permission to be included in the book. Other characters are fictional – although my brother did have a poodle called Zoe, and I did meet a Great Dane who became the model for Bonzo. Marmalade is a mixture of every ginger cat I have known.

I could not have written this book without a lot of support. My oldest friend, Helena, and her family suffered with considerable fortitude whilst I tried out passages on them. Dr Toni Hazell helped enormously with giving me a 'general practice' view of the problems of addiction. Miss Ella and Master Peter Hazell continually prodded me to keep writing as they wanted to know what Hugo was going to get up to next. My own family endured interminable phone calls whilst I read passages to them and encouraged me to continue. To all of them, a big thank you.

A big thank you is also due to Aunty Elly for looking after Hugo every Friday, as without that space I would never have had time to record Hugo's exploits from the previous week. To my colleague from RNLI days, Consultant Liaison Psychiatrist Dr Peter Aitken, for reviewing the MS and his kind words about it. To my old friend, Dr Chris Brooks, a thank you for also reviewing the MS and for making some very helpful comments about food addiction in the dog population of Rossendale, Lancashire. To Aunty and Uncle Herriot (they know who they are) for keeping Hugo alive after he ate half a kilo of chocolate. To Michael Rainey who so enthusiastically backed the book and whose energy helped it to fruition.

Thank you, all.

Introduction

My intent in writing Adventures with Hugo was to share with readers both sides of addiction through the eyes of Hugo, a food-addicted, rather humorous, rather chubby cockney Labrador. I hope that you will find this book entertaining – although addiction certainly isn't.

In my clinical practice I have observed how the difficulties that an addict has spread out and affect the lives of their nearest and dearest, as well as many beyond the bounds of the immediate family. Although Hugo is a rogue and is much-loved, the reality is that he is self-centred and ruled by his perennial quest for food; as much he loves his 'pack', food comes before anything else, and his life as an addict is chaotic.

The places in this book are real and you can enjoy walking around them in exactly the same way as Hugo and I did. The characters and events in this publication, other than those who gave their permission to be included, are fictitious, and any resemblance to actual persons, living or dead, is purely coincidental.

I hope this book brings a smile to its readers' faces, and also some understanding and comfort to those who may be affected by an addiction or an addict in their lives.

Labrador Blues

I wish I had opposable thumbs
It would sure help me to pick up crumbs
And open doors to snaffle tons
of lovely food
All I want is a great big steak
And humongous portions of chocolate cake
But all I get is an afternoon snooze
Oh, I got those Black Lab Blues

It's low-cal kibble for every meal
Since when was that the signed-for deal?
And I'm sure those scales are always set
At 'overweight' by my local vet
All I want is a great big steak
And humongous portions of chocolate cake
But all I get is an afternoon snooze
Oh, I got those Hungry Lab Blues

I've got to eat; it's in my genes
Breakfast, lunch and in betweens
Life is just a glorious quest
To find yet more for me tum to digest
All I want is a great big steak
And humongous portions of chocolate cake
But all I get is an afternoon snooze
Oh, I got those Black Lab Blues

Chapter 1

Introducing Hugo

The brown eyes did it. They followed the path of my hand from plate to mouth and back again. A muzzle settled on my thigh, from where the drool spread in a widening patch of damp across my jeans.

'It's my breakfast, not yours. You've already eaten.'

The patch of damp got bigger and the eyes became more pleading. I gave in and, in an instant, the corner of toast with just enough butter and thick-cut Robertson's marmalade to make it interesting, vanished. The muzzle was replaced in position and the eyes resumed scanning for movement between my plate and my hand.

This was now a part of my daily routine.

I had been living on my own in France, and feeling a little lost. My oldest friend came to my rescue: 'Why don't you come to London? I've got a spare room and you can write that book about your grandfather in World War One that you told me about.' It took almost no time to say yes. I put together enough clothes for a couple of months, locked up my house and came to England, expecting to spend a quiet and scholarly time writing.

It did not quite turn out that way, for, together with the room, came Hugo.

Hugo was a characterful, nine-year-old black Labrador who affected being much older than his years. He was slightly scruffy, in an endearing sort of way, as a previous skin complaint, and its curative medication, had left him with a thickened ruff of coat around his neck which, from some angles, made him look like a Victorian gent with "mutton-chop" whiskers. Every day seemed to be a permanent bad hair day for Hugo, and you could always tell his favourite sleeping places by little nests of black hair that required the strength of an industrial vacuum cleaner to remove. He took it all in his stride, with his customary amiable grin and a rather strange tail wag – a combination of side to side and hip-rolling. I came, later, to learn that Hugo attributed his appearance to one of his forbears having a night of passion with a Newfoundland; but, whatever his ancestry, Hugo was born a Londoner, and had that irrepressible attitude to life that is sometimes referred to as "the spirit of The Blitz". Hugo and I got on famously from the start and, to help my friend, I offered to take him for his daily walk on Hampstead Heath.

Hugo loved the Heath. The constant stream of walkers and picnickers offered him countless opportunities for food, and his amiable appearance and tail wag were frequently rewarded with a pat and a morsel. He seemed to have an uncanny ability to spot, and charm, other dog walkers who carried a supply of treats for their own pooch. Off he would go, ignoring their own dog, and introduce himself; in effect: Good morning, delighted to meet you. The name's Hugo. Bit short on breakfast this morning, haven't got a Winalot biscuit, have you? And with that, nine times out of ten, Hugo's affability would be rewarded. The charm of a walk, for Hugo, lay not so much in the opportunity for exercise and sniffs, as in the opportunity to undo his owner's attempts to keep him slim by grazing off handouts from passers-by.

Hugo had a big food problem. Labradors are, of course, famous for their food drive but, in Hugo's case, this had been elevated to an art form. He had learned not only to cadge biscuits from fellow dog walkers, but also to manipulate people to donate extra rations. Watching him work a group sitting on a park bench, having lunch, was like watching a master craftsman at his trade. The performance was polished by years of learning and was devastatingly effective. Several times I had to remind myself that I was, supposedly, responsible for him, when, in reality, I had become lost in admiration for his chutzpah.

At home he was a disaster. It was essential to keep food out of his reach, and any momentary lapse was immediately exploited. Even in his deepest sleeps, after food and exercise, it was impossible to open any cupboard, no matter how quietly, without finding him instantly by one's side. A delayed meal meant that nothing was safe – as a sorry trail of torn paper bag and tooth-punctured pieces of aluminium once bore witness. Of the tea lights there were no trace. Hugo showed no contrition. His face simply said, you were late, what did you expect?

He was one of those dogs who naturally acquired a retinue of followers. He was friendly with everybody at the local veterinary practice, and would saunter in to see the vet with pretty much the same attitude as somebody going to their London club. He adored his Aunty Elly, who looked after him when his mistress went away, and he treated me like a long-lost friend who was always dim enough to stand him lunch because he'd left his wallet behind. Hugo had one real dog friend: PJ. PJ was an occasional visitor, and worked as a guide dog for a blind friend of Hugo's mistress. Hugo's relationship with PJ was slightly one of awe, for PJ was many things that Hugo wasn't; he was slimmer, less food-driven, more self-controlled, and tended to treat Hugo with that slight disdain that a town dog has for one from the country, despite the fact that their homes were, actually, the other way around.

Hugo's sleeping arrangements had evolved over time. During the day he occupied a bed in the kitchen from where he could observe the human traffic between the cooker, fridge and larder. At night, when everyone went to bed, he would take up position on a bed on the landing, and would stay there until he was satisfied that everyone was asleep and there was no further possibility of a night-time snack. Then he would steal downstairs, nose open the study door, and curl up on a small sofa from where he could observe the front and back doors and the staircase. It was as if he had taken up lodgings in a castle guardroom. Here he would sleep until about half past three in the morning. Then he would set out on his pre-dawn patrol to see if any members of his pack were awake and, if so, present them with a half-eaten sock or a toy zebra. His nocturnal present-giving always produced the cry of 'Go to bed!' and he would grumpily retire to the landing, with many sighs and long bouts of simulated snoring. Eventually, around 6.00am, he would win and be given his "first breakfast" – his morning pills for his arthritis encased in a triangle of Laughing Cow cream cheese – and be let out into the garden to see off any foxes that had, injudiciously, remained.

Hugo was unlike other dogs that I had met. I struggled to put my finger on the difference, but he seemed more independent, more self-contained, not quite such a pack animal. He appeared to watch the world with amused interest, and his food drive wasn't always just begging but had elements of a showman's act. By his actions, I would catch him displaying real insight into human behaviour. I didn't just enjoy his company, I felt myself spending increasing amounts of time observing him in the same way that I was beginning, somewhat worryingly, to feel that he was observing me.

Our walks were a constant source of entertainment and I treasured the time we spent together. Hugo very definitely had a mind of his own, and if he had eaten what he regarded as an "adequate" breakfast, nothing would induce him to walk further than the top of the road. Attempts to tug his lead were met with a withering look, and four paws firmly planted in resistance on the ground. Changing direction to home always resulted in a bouncy quickstep, however, and the resumption of his customary bonhomie. On other days, he wouldn't be interested in walking at all, and would look at you, from his bed, with glazed eyes and a vacant stare, like a '60's rock star after a bad night.

We were on our third walk together when something very strange happened. Hugo, who had always been either well ahead or well behind, came to walk by my side. Suddenly, I heard a voice:

'Something bovvering you, guv?'

I looked around. Nothing to be seen.

'Something bovvering you, guv?'

I looked down. 'Hugo. You can speak?'

'Didn't me mistress tell you?'

'No, and I wouldn't have believed it either.'

'Really. I've heard you tell her that after a lifetime in medicine nothing would surprise you.'

'This does. You really can talk?'

'Obviously, but with a bit of an accent.'

'I'd already noticed.'

'Not quite what you think. Us dogs have floppy tongues so we struggle wiv "ths". It's when you put your tongue up at the back of your teeth to make the "th" sound. Linguists call it a "voiced dental non-sibilant fricative". Double-Dutch to me. Anyway, I'm a talking therapist Labrador.'

'Therapist Labrador?'

'Of course,' he said. 'You've heard of guide dogs for the blind, hearing dogs and helping dogs. Well, some of us – a very select few, mark you – get to be therapist dogs. Big difference is we don't start our training as puppies. We have to have life experience. Take me, for example. I was deprived as a kid, rarely taken for a walk – although I took me own when I could get away. I developed a serious eating disorder. I have a real problem with food; could call it an addiction, I suppose. Anyway, always hungry, and always totally distracted at the prospect of food. Interferes with me therapy sessions, if you get me drift. You will normally get me undivided attention unless food gets in the way. I suffer so badly I even react to words that start with food. Take "exactly" for example.'

'Exactly?'

'Yes. Trouble is, not many people say exactly. Mostly they say eggsactly – and that's it. Immediately I smell omelettes, soft-boiled eggs, eggs Benedict, eggs Royale, eggs Florentine and such like. The whole Carluccio's breakfast menu swims before me eyes and me mind just wanders and I start drooling.

Therapy goes out the window. So, say what you like, but just be careful with your words and pronunciation. . .' Hugo paused. 'Well,' he continued, 'like a lot of addicts, I eventually went into therapy. Learnt how to deal with me issues. It's good to talk 'n that. Ultimately, I decided to pass on me experience to others, like yourself, so I went for me therapy dog training.'

'It doesn't seem to have helped with your food drive, Hugo.'

'Certainly has, guv, you should have seen me before. Now, although you're a medical man, you seem to have got things on your mind, and since I haven't got anything better to do I thought I might take you on as a patient. Take it or leave it, really. Anyway, me mistress thought I might help.'

'She didn't tell me anything about this.'

'Probably thought it might come as a pleasant surprise.'

'How did you learn to speak?'

'Same way as anybody else. Listening and practice.'

'I'm still astonished. A talking therapist Labrador. Your offer of help does seem a bit condescending, though. Sure you can spare the time?'

'Don't be sarcastic, guv, it doesn't suit you. There was I, opening up about me past and me afflictions, and all you can do is use cheap humour. If we're to make progress you've got to learn to be a bit respectful and think of me feelings. Let's get some ground rules going. I have a different therapy model to everyone else: you listen, I observe and talk, and then you feed me. In return you gets the benefit of me wisdom and accumulated life experience. Now, if you don't mind, let's get on with the walk. I think you've done enough today just getting your head round the idea of a therapist Labrador.'

And with that Hugo was gone, distracted by the remnant smells of a picnic on a park bench. For the first time, in a long time, a smile crossed my face. With a therapist Labrador, life was going to be rather different.

Our fourth walk took us up onto Hampstead Heath and into the grounds of Kenwood. This was one of Hugo's favourite jaunts in the summer, as he was able to browse through a better quality of food litter. He seemed to have a particular liking for Pret A Manger wrappers, having once found a packet with a completely untouched crayfish and rocket sandwich. I had expected him to talk again but, instead, he just rootled around in his normal way, inspecting waste bins and passers-by for any prospect of food.

As we came up to the house, he darted off, having spied a dropped ice cream cone. Licking his lips as he returned he said, 'I'm a complete sucker for blackcurrant and clotted cream. So, what's been the problem?'

'Oh, this and that. Don't much want to talk about it, anyway. It's one of those things that will settle with time and distance.'

'Right, guv, I suggest we sit on that park bench over there and we'll have a chat and I'll have a little lie down in the shade. Haven't got any Bonios, have you? Always think better with a Bonio.'

'Sadly, no, Hugo. But I'll see what I can do later.'

We sat on the bench, looking south out over the Heath and down to the city.

'Always liked this view.'

'One of the best in London.'

'Know London well, guv?'

'I was born here. There are bits I know very well.'

'Sure you don't want to talk?'

'Not at the moment, no.'

Hugo looked at me thoughtfully. 'A Bonio would help, even a Winalot.'

'Who for?'

'Me.'

'I haven't got anything.'

'Nothing.'

'No.'

'Not even a fiver so we can have tea in the cafe?'

'As it happens, yes, but . . .'

Hugo was gone in a flash, his lead trailing behind, and I only just caught up with him by the café terrace.

'What was that all about?'

'Didn't want you to change your mind. Now, slip the end of me lead under the chair leg and I'll keep the table for you, it looks better that way. There should be a bowl of water sculling around here somewhere if you wouldn't mind fetching it. Dirtier the better, improves the taste. Can't stand fresh tap water. Whilst you're at the counter, mine's a ham sandwich.'

'Any other instructions? I'm not used to being at a Labrador's beck and call.'

'Don't mind me, spent a lot of time with a cat friend of mine, some of his attitude must have rubbed off. You know what they say, "Dogs have owners, cats have staff".'

I found the water, added a few leaves for good measure, and left it with Hugo. After a quick drink he sprawled out with the bowl beside him. I went to get tea.

'Where's me ham sandwich?'

'On the tray, just wait while I unwrap it.'

'You could just toss it down.'

'Let's be civilised.'

'Hmm, if we're going to be civilised you can undo me lead now. By the way, guv, not a word about this to 'Er Ladyship.'

'And she is?'

'Me owner, me mistress. "Babi" as her grandchildren call her. Helena, your friend. Cor, you ain't half slow.'

'And why should I keep this secret?'

"She's trying to keep me weight down, perennial problem. Don't get me wrong, I like me Obesity Management for dogs food, but a bit of variety is always welcome. I'll let you into a secret, guv: she likes giving her grandchildren little treats; you treat me the same way and we'll have a capital time.'

You're a rascal,' I said, handing him his sandwich.

'Yes,' he said, unapologetically, 'and an addict, currently sort of in recovery. Been a food addict most of me life. It's in me genes, you know.'

'I had heard. I also heard, the nicer the Labrador, the more they are likely to be addicted.'

Hugo looked up at me. 'That's perfectly true, and we always seem to be around addicts. Bit like most people, I suppose. Everybody knows at least one addict. My cat friend Marmalade had a big problem with catnip, and if it weren't for Bonzo . . .'

'Bonzo?'

'Another friend of mine, a Great Dane with an attitude problem, who keeps us both in check, somehow. You'll meet him someday. Even me Aunt Ethel had a problem – not that she was addicted herself. She were living with a couple in London. Media types they were. You know the sort. Very precious, high levels of anxiety, and lots of liquor. Right palaver it were living there. One moment all lovey-dovey, next moment all hell breaks loose. Aunt Ethel had a terrible time. Her job were checking the Aga were working. Quite responsible really, on account of the fact that, except for meal breaks, she had to keep her nose against it all day to check it hadn't gone out – it was a bit old and dodgy you see.

"'Well," Aunt Ethel says to me, "you should just have seen 'em. Go out to work in the morning, and a nice quiet day. Then the master comes home, pours himself a glass of wine – a big one mind, you know, sort of a quarter of a bottle size – and starts telling her what sort of a day he's had. No conversation, just a monologue. Next thing, he's still talking and had a second glass, and he not having had any food or anything. The lady of the house is getting a bit fed up now, because he's been talking non-stop for the last half hour and she wants to offload too. He gets a bit pointed, she takes umbrage, and next thing you know words have been said and an atmosphere descends on the house.

"'D'you know what?" says Aunt Ethel. "What then happens is that they start drinking again and sniping at each other, and the original reason for the bad feelings is forgotten and they start dragging up old personal stuff between them. They have a half-hearted attempt at making some supper, but it all goes wrong because they aren't paying attention and they start shouting again.

"'Trouble is," says Ethel, "I'd met this before. Previous house I was in there were all sorts of problems and they ended up going their separate ways. Even had a battle over me. Eventually, they compromised and sent me to live with their best friends. Didn't know what they were letting me in for."

Hugo's attention switched. A couple had just finished their food and were about to put the remains in a bin. In a flash, Hugo was beside them with the starving-Labrador-look on his face. Before I could call him back he took the remnants of the pesto and mozzarella wrap and consumed it in a gulp. With a profuse wag of his tail he thanked them and ambled back to me.

'Now where was I, Oh yes, Aunt Ethel. It's very difficult really. She says to me, "How could I hand in me notice? I'd grown to love them. They always looked after me, kept me warm, gave me food – mark you, meals weren't always regular and that's a big thing for a Labrador. Most of the time it was OK, but then he'd have a drink or two and next thing mealtime is missed. He'd always remember though, eventually, and sometimes you'd get your normal meal, generally splurged across the floor as he put it down, or you'd get leftovers because he couldn't remember where the dog food was kept. Leftovers were interesting." Cold curry was Aunt Ethel's favourite . . .' Hugo paused. 'I like curry too. D'you know, guv, you can almost measure how much I like different foods by the amount of drool I produce.'

'I'd already noticed, Hugo. Curry seems to come top, just above tomato and basil sauce with grated parmesan.'

'Blimey, you are observant for a human. I remember once finding an opened, uneaten chicken biryani dropped outside a takeaway. I'd been really hungry that day, walking the streets after running away from home. Takeaways were always a magnet for me; I could follow the smell for miles as the spices carried on the street air.' Hugo shook himself. 'Doesn't do any good thinking about food like that. I just end up completely gripped by the need to eat. Never get anything done that way. Bad for me health you might say.'

'Now, guv, Aunt Ethel. She quite enjoyed the leftovers, made a change from the unchanging monotony of normal dogfood. Trouble for her was the unpredictability. She never knew where she was. One moment life was normal, great fun, with: "Come on, Ethel, forget the Aga, let's go for a walk," or "Come here, Ethel, have a cuddle with me on the sofa," and then the next moment it's back to shouting and tears. Poor old Aunt Ethel didn't know what to do. She'd find a corner to lie in, try not to be noticed, and hope she didn't become part of the row. She had to go in the end. One unhappy person she could have coped with, but not two. Us dogs like happy packs, doesn't do us any good to be caught up in conflict.'

Hugo sniffed and caught the residue of drool from when he had been thinking about chicken biryani. He was a soft-hearted Labrador, and he hated to think that Aunt Ethel had been unhappy.

He then got up and sat down beside me and leaned into my leg for contact. I reached forward and stroked his head as the café staff started to clear the tables.

'It's a funny old world,' Hugo remarked. 'Nothing is ever quite what it seems. Ethel thought she was going to a lovely house, and really looked forward to spending her time in front of the Aga. She'd met the couple before and they'd seemed ever so nice. Really upset she was.'

'What happened to her, Hugo?'

'She was an old dog, you know. She came to live with me mum and us for a bit, but she didn't last long before she passed over . . .' He paused again. 'Guv,' he said, 'sure you haven't got a Bonio?'

We walked home.

Chapter 2

Coram Fields

Hugo was in great spirits the next day. Rising early, he dashed to the back door and then to his breakfast bowl. He then sauntered over as I was making coffee.

'Fancy a trip out, guv?'

'Where to, Hugo?'

'Thought of taking you down to Coram Fields. Wanted to show you where the Foundling Hospital was and talk a bit about my childhood.'

'I thought Thomas Coram and the Foundling Hospital was before your time, Hugo?'

'Of course it was, guv. But it's kind of symbolic, you know. A useful backdrop to me thoughts.'

'I'll get ready, Hugo, we can take the Tube. We can change at Kings Cross and get on the Piccadilly–'

Hugo suddenly groaned and started to drool. 'Guv,' he said, 'I've asked you to be careful about your language when it comes to food, I've got pictures in me head of hot dogs, burgers–'

'Why, Hugo?'

'Piccadilly, guv, it sounds like piccalilli, and everything in my head is suddenly smothered in yellow and tasting fantastic!'

The puddle of drool on the floor grew bigger and Hugo groaned again.

'I'm so sorry, Hugo, can I help? I'm a bit concerned, though. Don't you think you need more therapy yourself if the very mention of a Tube line puts you in this state?'

'Guv, it's work in progress. I've learnt to deal with most of me triggers, but this is a bad one.'

And with that Hugo groaned again, and again and the puddle of drool grew bigger. Thinking that the only thing I could do was distract him from what was evidently a very traumatic stimulus, I said, 'Hugo, we could have a second breakfast. There is a Pret A Manger near Holborn, which is on the Central Line. I could buy you a sundried tomato, mayo and egg baguette, if you like?'

The transformation was immediate. Hugo sat up.

'Guv you're a diamond. I can cope with that. Was a bit afraid just then I was going to drown in me own drool.'

And with that episode behind us we set off on our journey, taking care to keep our eyes averted as we passed the signs for the 'Piccalilli' Line at Holborn. I made a mental note never to travel with him on the Bakerloo!

Arriving at Holborn, we duly made our way to Pret. Whilst we had our second breakfast I realised another difference between Hugo and other dogs: he sometimes savoured his food. No inevitable bolting down in a couple of gulps, but a leisurely dismantling of his baguette, with the filling neatly scooped out in a couple of rolls of his tongue, and then the baguette lovingly treated as a soft, indulgent chew.

We sat in companionable silence at one of the pavement tables, watching the world go by. After a while, we walked up into Grays Inn Road. Hugo led the way, keeping a beady eye out for food opportunities. I was very impressed by his ability to navigate around London.

'Have you done the Knowledge?'

Hugo looked up. 'What?'

'The Knowledge. The cabbies test of getting around London streets.'

Hugo gave me a despairing look.

'Guv, us dogs do it by smell. Every part of London has a different smell. Now, take Coram Fields. Kiddies play area. Adults only admitted with a child. Mums and nannies go there to push prams and let tots have a safe run around. Consequence: borne on the wind is an ever so faint smell of nappies. It's an easy place to find. The other help is what I call "paw memory". Once you've trotted around a few times and found somewhere from different directions, it just becomes ingrained in you. Sheep have that, you know.'

'Sheep?'

'Yes. I was talking to an old sheep dog once. He'd worked up in the Lake District. "Hugo," he said, "you wouldn't believe how tricky sheep get, they know every nook and cranny of a mountainside and pass it down through the generations. It's called hefting. They get hefted to their territory." I was interested in that. I always thought hefting meant working out how much something weighed. Apparently, same word two different meanings. Got me interested in words that did.'

We carried on up to Coram Fields and stopped outside the Foundling Museum.

Hugo cleared his throat and began. 'I was born,' he said, somewhat pompously, 'in Bermondsey. You could say as how me food problems started there because we was right next door to the old Peek Freane biscuit factory. Can you imagine, guv, lying in the back yard of your house and smelling the Garibaldi's, Pearls, Bourbons, Golden Puffs and shortcake being made. Some days it was Cheeselets; that was me favourite. A real trial for a young Labrador puppy it was, you know how exuberant we are. Nowadays, they make adverts about us pulling loo rolls around; but back in the old days we spent all our time trying to scrump the reject biscuits.

'Happy days, but it didn't do anything for me waistline. Me brothers and sisters used to call me Little Portly – that's an affectionate diminutive in case you didn't know, guv, on account of me shape. Mark you, it was a bit of a case of the pot calling the kettle black, because they were all just as bad as me.

'Dad weren't much help. He used to egg us on and made Mum fair mad at him. He weren't much use me dad. Bit of a roamer. Thought our education finished with learning how to forage and live on the streets. When we were very young, he used to watch Mum trying to teach us manners and morals and where you could politely do your business. When we grew up a bit he took over and said, "You've had enough of that now. You need to learn how to live in the real world." Used to really upset me mum. Then there'd be a row, and then he'd get a bit handy with his paws and teeth. He used to frighten all of us, including Mum. Never taught us about love and loyalty. Wasn't a role model to us. Quite strange in a Labrador. Only met one like that again and he was a bad dog, really bad.

'Looking back, I can see it now. Me dad was an angry dog. Angry inside. Could really have made something of himself but couldn't escape his own past. He never had much.

From what he told me, his mum were angry and his dad were weak. He was brought up to be angry with everybody. Not much love and affection, and it showed. We all need love and affection. Thing is, Dad had a lot of character and charm and we all followed his example. Trouble was, because of his temper and unpredictability, we all grew up afraid in one way or another. It was better after he left. Mum had more influence then, but some of the damage he'd done to us persisted. Mum was always sad inside. The world weighed terrible on her shoulders but she did her best by us. Funny how problems come down the generations.

'Anyway, me mum decided she couldn't cope in Bermondsey. That was after me brother Fred died of an overdose of dark chocolate "suggestives". We begged him not to eat 'em. "Fred," we said, "remember dogs and chocolate don't mix," but he would have none of it, thought he was immune and it wouldn't happen to him; trouble is, it did. There's a lesson in that, guv, it's easy to believe the bad stuff won't happen to you but, if you put yourself in harm's way, sooner or later it will. Me poor old mum took it bad and moved us all. "Hugo," she said, "it's too much temptation. I remember what it was like being a young Labrador with an ongoing battle with food addiction, it took a lot of training and constant attention to me diet to stay slim. There's no hope for any of you if we stay next to a biscuit factory." And with that she ups and moves us.

'Well,' went on Hugo, 'she takes us to a new place in Walthamstow. Walthamstow! That were a real problem, because north and south of the river are very different places. Had to keep very quiet about where we'd come from in case of trouble. Manby Road it were – although they've changed the name now to Tenby Road. Can't think why they'd do that, no connections to Tenby, and the only good thing about it were the playing fields and the reservoir. I learnt to swim there, although always had terrible trouble with the waterworks inspector. He didn't approve of us going for a swim, but we were Labradors, what else do you expect? He'd shout at us from the bank, but we would just swim to the other side and amble off. Wouldn't recommend it, though, water was cold, even though we are, what you might call, "equipped by nature" for activity like that.

'It was a bit boring in Manby Road. I missed the smells of Bermondsey, and the food opportunities were right down. Dad had gone by then, and Mum couldn't afford for us to go into training, so we all started to roam. A couple of me brothers and sisters were sold, but the money wasn't much and it didn't last long. Me brother Edward struck lucky, he was always the best-looking of us, and the lady that bought him sold him on to a visiting American, who took him to California. Dead jealous I was, all those beaches and surfing and supersized portions, without having to ask. By the end of the year there was only me, Arthur – me younger brother – Ethel, me sister – she was named after me mum's sister by the way – and that's when it happened.'

Hugo started to sniff and sob uncontrollably.

'What happened, Hugo?' I asked quietly.

'It were terrible, guv. Arthur and me had wandered off and were inspecting the bins behind a greengrocers for anything edible. All of a sudden, this van comes round the corner and hits Arthur just as he was moving on to another bin. Not even time for a yelp, and that was it. Stone-dead. Mum and me was beside ourselves, but that weren't the worst of it. Three weeks later, Mum gets a telegram saying that me brother Bill was also dead. He'd found a home with a ship's captain, but he'd run off when they got to Melbourne to try his luck in Australia. Don't know what did for him, but he was found on a street corner starving, and they were too late to save him. It finished poor old Mum. From seven of us she was down to two, Ethel and me, and by this time neither of us were, what you might call, respectable.'

Hugo continued through his sniffs.

'Poor old Mum went into a real decline after that, and six months later she left Ethel and me for the big dog kennel in the sky. And then, to cap it all, Ethel runs off with this flash border collie she'd just met and goes to live in a pub. Well, that were it, I was on me own. You might say as how I'd become a foundling, which was why I brought you here, guv.'

Hugo's sniffs subsided, but his mood was sombre, and he sat dejectedly for a while looking around him. He caught sight of a small boy chasing his sister, and it seemed to lift him; perhaps he was thinking of he and Ethel in happier times. He turned around to look at me.

'Didn't know what to do then. Mum 'ad gone, Ethel weren't interested in her brother anymore, and I was left to me own devices. Being young and fairly fit I was able to look after myself for a bit, but I missed having a pack. The area round Walthamstow was a pretty rough area for a Labrador. Plenty of pit bulls and such like, but I was the only Lab. Wasn't safe to stay around, so I gradually mooched west. Ended up in Soho eventually. Loved that, full of colour and life. It felt safer with more people around. Out east it was scary at night. Streets were empty mostly, but you never knew what was around the corner. You'd be shivering on a doorstep somewhere, trying to get to sleep, and then you'd hear a snarl and a frightened yelp and that was it. Soho was much better. All sorts were there. We all got along and there was much less aggravation.'

We had walked north, up Judd Street. We crossed the Euston Road by the British Library and up into Camden Town. Our route eventually took us back on to the Heath, and we veered across to Highgate Ponds, where we sat watching the ducks for a while. Hugo was lost in thought, and an occasional sob still shook him as he remembered his siblings.

'Reckon it was the heat that got to Bill,' he said. 'Clue is in being a Labrador. It's cold in Labrador, and we all definitely thrived when it was chilly. Can't really take the sun. I like it, but I heat up really quickly if I lay out in it and have to go and find a nice cold floor to cool down on. When you've nowhere to go but a hot pavement, it must have been terrible. And as for Arthur, he was as enthusiastic about his foraging for food as he was terrible at keeping a lookout; reckon that's what done for him.'

Hugo sobbed again and turned his attention to the ducks.

'Doesn't do to dwell on things, guv, but it's hard not to.' He sat dejectedly, watching as two ducks squabbled over a piece of bread. 'Can we go home, guv, I've had enough of today.'

'I was about to suggest it, you didn't have to tell me, you know.'

'Thing is, guv, some things hurt so much they never go away. Now, you can try and bury them, but they keep on coming back so that doesn't work, so, when they bother you, it's worth being honest about them. They taught me that in therapy school.'

'I know, Hugo. I've seen some very bad things, which kept popping up in my head. I used to imagine I had left luggage lockers inside my head, and when a bad memory recurred I would imagine putting it in a locker and closing the door and turning the key on it.'

'Did it work?'

'No, the doors would open of their own accord, and off I would go on the not-so-merry-go-round again.'

'How d'you deal with it?'

'I had some therapy, Hugo. It really helped a lot. But I also worked hard at how I looked at life.'

'We must talk about it, guv, compare notes, but I've had enough today. I feel really drained and I need a good long kip.'

We walked on, up past Kenwood, across to the Spaniards Inn and down onto the Heath Extension. To add to the general feeling of gloom and despondency, the rain started. Eventually, we got home, more than a little wet. After a thorough towel down and a well-deserved meal, Hugo collapsed onto his bed and fell deeply asleep. The occasional sniff and sob, and the periodic twitch and woof, told me that he was still reliving his story in his dreams. I tiptoed out of the room and left him to it.

Chapter 3

Picnic Snaffling

Hugo was subdued for the next few days, but gradually a semblance of his normal good humour returned and we planned another day out. We decided to avoid using the Underground and, at Hugo's suggestion, we took the bus. Somewhat tongue in cheek, I suggested we could take the bus to Ealing Broadway and then to Sandpits Road on the way to Kingston.

Hugo looked at me despairingly.

'You trying to wind me up, guv?' he said. 'The route to Ham House trick. I'll have you know that when I was in therapy they tried that, and Pudding Lane, as well as "How about a trip to Ruislip?"'.

Hugo was clearly upset and I forbore to mention that if he could cope with these names he should not have such a problem with the Piccalilli Line. I decided that I would have to talk to him about this, but now was clearly not the time.

To ease matters we compromised on the bus to Hyde Park Corner.

'You know,' said Hugo, as we sat on the upper deck of the bus, 'I only have a problem with that Tube line name.'

'What, the one we mustn't mention, rather like actors avoid referring to Macbeth in case it brings them bad luck? They refer to it as the "Scottish" play.'

'Just so, guv. That's not a bad name for it; perhaps we should call it the Scottish Line. Now I know when we get off we could walk up Piccadilly itself, but I reckon I've done that so many times it doesn't affect me anymore. Triggers can be quite irrational. Anyway, I rather like it there, the streets have nice names like Half Moon Street.'

'You must have seen a lot of London when you were a foundling, Hugo?'

'It was hard being on me own. Us dogs are pack animals, and we don't do being on our own very well. Need someone to team up with. I tried down at the Waterloo underpasses, but I found it scary, all that noise and bare concrete. And some of the characters you met, well . . . after a bit I tried up in Soho, as you know. Much better.

'There was a cat there who became a really great friend. Marmalade colour she was, I told you about her yesterday, and that's what we called her. She was as mad as a hatter. She used to live in a lamp shop near the top of Berwick Street in Soho. Shop is closed now, such a shame. W. Sitch and Co. it were called. Marmalade used to sit in the window watching the world go by. She saw me go by one day and came out to say hello. "Look like you need a warm up," she said, and took me through to the workshop at the back. What a place, floor to ceiling with brass lamps. Didn't seemed to have changed inside since Dickens was writing. "Been going since 1776," said Marmalade proudly. Many is the hour we spent sitting by the hearth in the back telling stories. I loved that place. Full of atmosphere and mystery it was. Owners were proper diamonds and always made a fuss of us. Only place I knew that really felt like home. I can't tell you how much I enjoyed it. That was where Marmalade introduced me to Bonzo. We'd been discussing the difficulty of emptying some of the new bins behind restaurants. I'd found I couldn't push 'em over. It was Marmalade who came up with the solution.

"'It's physics, Hugo," she said. "We need a bigger dog to push at the top and you to act as a fulcrum." Had me completely confused. At first, I thought she was talking about some type of bread I hadn't heard of: full crumb. Anyway, I said, you may remember, but I didn't go to school, what are you talking about? Well, she just sighed and gave me one of those "cat" looks; you know, the sort that say, you dogs will never get it.

"'Hugo, you just stand with your four paws firmly planted on the pavement – you can do that, can't you?" she said. "And my friend Bonzo can push the bin up against you, put his paws up at the top of the bin and tumble it over you. Then you can both grab a bit of leftovers whilst I keep watch."

'That was the beginning of a glorious partnership. Bonzo, Marmalade and me. The three bears had nothing on us – though I do share their fondness for porridge. Trouble was, Marmalade got addicted to catnip. There weren't much around where she was, and her forays to find it became longer and longer. Eventually, she left the shop and lived rough down at the Chelsea Physic Garden. "Hugo," she used to say, "best quality catnip in London, come down here and try it, it'll really tune you out." Well, guv, I figured I had enough problems with food without being cross-addicted to catnip. But she were a lovely cat, unbelievably laid back, very fond of her I am, it were terrible seeing her decline. Caught up with her again later, but that were another story. You'll meet 'em both sometime, they're always around here.

'Anyway, the first thing I needed were to find somewhere proper to doss down. I had a spot of luck running into a props man at a theatre near Wardour Street. He had a soft spot for Labs and he used to let me in the back door after everybody had gone home. I could always find a cosy nook to settle down to sleep. Could be a bit spooky sometimes, though, with some of the theatre sets. Occasionally, the night watchman would play with the thunder machine. That were a good way of spoiling me sleep. All those cannonballs rolling around.

'The cleaning staff used to share their breakfast with me in the morning, and then I'd pop over the road to the pub and have a second meal. After that it was back on the streets for the day. That was the beginning of me serious addiction, because there was always food in the bins at the back of the cafés and restaurants. It were quite an education, too. Not many dogs get a chance to try a cuisine as varied as you find in Soho. Personally, I developed a taste for Argentinian – great steaks when you could get one, but it didn't happen very often. Chinese was always more reliable for leftovers, as customers always over ordered. Not sure about prawn crackers, though. They used to get stuck in me teeth. Still, it were grub. Could always force it down.'

'Hugo,' I said, 'you amaze me. You have a completely different insight into the economics of the restaurant business.'

'Well, guv,' said Hugo, adopting his slightly pompous expert look, 'took what you might call a "professional interest" as a bin emptier because, other than hanging out with some of me mates, there wasn't a lot to do. Got to have a sense of purpose in life, if you get me drift, even if it is only as a food critic.

'It was an interesting time, as because you're a Labrador, people don't think you're a stray. Us Labs have a bit of class. Whenever the dog warden was about, all you had to do was walk smartly at heel beside some well-dressed gent and the warden took no notice at all. Other poor dogs had it tougher. If you looked a bit scruffy, or looked as if you'd been sleeping rough, you got targeted. Sooner or later you'd get scooped up and taken to the pound. Lost a lot of my friends that way.'

Hugo paused. The faraway look had come into his eyes as he relived unpleasant times in his past.

'Was it much of a problem?' I asked gently.

'It varied. As a posh breed, and being quick-witted and resourceful, you could generally get away with it; but if you were just an ordinary run-of-the-mill mongrel you had a terrible time. Mark you, even them was luckier than the terriers and mastiffs. Any suggestion you were the sort that was looking for a punch-up and your card was marked big time. Other thing for the mastiffs was, however nice they were, you didn't want to be around 'em or you would get noticed too. Made for a lonely time for 'em. They didn't last long on the streets. Shame though, there were some real diamonds amongst 'em. They were victims of prejudice really.'

'How so?'

'Well, guv, don't know if you've noticed, but people see what they expect to see. So, if you're a mastiff, the dog wardens immediately see trouble. They don't stop and think. They just see trouble. It was as if they said to themselves, "Hello, here comes a mastiff, there's going to be trouble." It's psychology really. You sees what you expects to see, not what's actually there. It's not right, but it's the way we're wired. It's lazy thinking really. You've got to make the effort to see what is reality. Thing is, we know it's wrong to think carelessly. We've got phrases in language like, "You mustn't judge a book by its cover" or "All that glistens isn't gold". Them phrases tell us you must look and think about things and not just make assumptions. Trouble is, that takes effort. Unless you get used to doing it all the time, it's too easy to go with your prejudices. They taught me about that in therapy school.'

By this time, we had got to Hyde Park Corner. We got off the bus and Hugo looked around.

'Could do with stretching me legs,' he said. 'Can we go into the park?'

As we entered, a squirrel was busy burying acorns. Hugo stopped to watch.

'Clever little blighters, aren't they, guv? I admire their foresight, putting food away for the winter; don't know how they remember where they put it, though. Personally, I believe in eating when you can and putting faith in blagging me next meal if there isn't any forage. It's always worked for me.'

Losing interest, Hugo wandered on.

'Didn't come here much in the past. They were stricter on strays in the Royal parks; thought we lowered the tone of the place, I expect. Cats did better. Marmalade used to say, "Hugo, nothing beats a park. Any sign of trouble and you can hide up a tree and pretend you're a leopard." Thing was, neither Bonzo nor me could ever spot her against the grass. We thought she were brilliant at hiding. Couldn't understand why she would want to go up a tree. Turned out that Bonzo and me were colour blind. All of the humans could see her clearly. Know what nearly did for her in the end?'

'No?'

'Well, she found this pot of catnip growing on a roof terrace. Got absolutely sent by it and fell off. Fell four floors, poor little thing.'

'I'm so sorry, Hugo. I know she meant a lot to you.'

'She didn't die, guv, she fell onto an awning and just lay there glassy-eyed saying, "I am a leopard, I'm a leopard," until they took her away to a cat centre. They sussed her catnip addiction out straight away and rehomed her in the north of Scotland, where they could only grow catnip in a cold frame. Poor little girl, she was such fun. Had a wonderful purr, and a tongue like sandpaper. Anyway, after her deportation to the freezin' north, as it were, she thought, I can't be having this. Do you know what she did?'

'No?'

'She managed to escape, and then stowed away on the Inverness to London sleeper train. Reckon as how she had been to too many performances of "Cats" and thought of herself as Skimbleshanks. We'd all given up hope of seeing her again, and then, one day, there she were again, all bright and breezy. I was ever so pleased to see her. By the time she got back she seemed to have got over her catnip addiction too. After that we was inseparable for a while.'

Hugo pushed away some leaves and dug up the acorn the squirrel had just buried. He looked puzzled.

'Don't know how you get through a winter on these,' he said. 'Can you imagine, four months on a diet of damp nuts? Gives me the shivers. Reminds me of the Norwegians. They pack trout in tubs for up to a year and then eat it when it's fermented. Call it rakfisk, apparently. Remarkable. Why would you want to wait that long before eating a good bit o' fish?'

He buried the nut again. He looked around.

'I dunno. Nuts if you're a squirrel; whatever you can get from dabbling if you're a duck. Makes me pleased to be a Labrador. I know you've got me on light rations, but at least I get a bit of salami or the odd biryani from time to time, but nuts day after day . . .' His voice died away disconsolately.

A Great Dane wandered down the path towards us. Hugo recognised him instantly and, after the customary exchange of sniffs, they raced off, barking happily and went to ground behind a tea hut. I went over to check, and they looked up somewhat shiftily as I rounded the corner.

Hugo cleared his throat nervously. 'Guv, meet Thor. Stupid name really; some nod to his Viking ancestry, I suppose. Best to call him Bonzo, that's what his friends do. He's the mate I told you about.'

'Pleased to meet you, Bonzo,' I said, slightly anxiously.

Bonzo looked friendly enough, but he was built like a Viking and carried himself with the self-assurance of knowing it. I wasn't sure I would want to cross him. I reached into my pocket for a Winalot.

'I'll have that, guv,' said Hugo, snaffling the biscuit before I could give it to his friend. 'Bonzo's given 'em up for Lent, 'aven't you, mate. And, in any case, he doesn't have the food drive of a Labrador.'

Bonzo looked on silently, waiting to take his cue from Hugo.

Hugo turned to me. 'Couldn't give us five minutes could you, guv? Got a few things to reminisce over.'

I looked at the pair of them. There was definitely something going on and I wasn't quite sure what to do. Rather against my better judgement I said, 'OK, Hugo, I'll be on the park bench over there. Don't be long.'

Ten minutes later Hugo reappeared on his own.

'What was that all about?' I enquired.

'Blast from my slightly shady past,' said Hugo, looking rather embarrassed. 'Not very proud of it.'

'Oh yes?'

'Well, Bonzo, Marmalade and me used to work this act. We'd find a family having a picnic on the Heath, I'd do my soppy Labrador act with the kids, letting them stroke me and pat me, and I'd gradually edge them away from their adults. Time would come when the kids would be called back, but of course they didn't listen, they were having such a good time. Then the adults would get up to come and get 'em and, as soon as their backs were turned, Bonzo would nip in and help 'imself to as much of the picnic as he could carry. Marmalade would act as lookout. Then the three of us would find somewhere private and enjoy our lunch.'

'Hugo, I'm shocked.'

'So you should be, guv. Not very proud of it myself, but it worked a treat. Mind you, the absolute master at charming kids was an English springer, name of Sam. Black and white he was, looked like a French aristocrat. He'd teamed up with a rescue greyhound. Thing is, the act only works if the thieving one is a picky eater, like Bonzo. Wouldn't work with two Labs, for instance. There'd you be, enticing the kids, your mate goes in for the "lift", and by the time you've met up he's got hiccups because he's bolted the grub, has an embarrassed grin on his face and is saying, "Terribly sorry, Hugo, couldn't help it."

Had a few fights over that until I learnt how important it is to have the right partner.'

'What made you give up?'

Hugo looked thoughtful.

'Combination of finding religion and doing the "twelve-paws" – a variation on the twelve-step program for humans learning to manage addiction. But that took rather a long time. When you're on your own you've got to survive, guv. It's all very well having that inner conscience that says, Hugo, me lad, you shouldn't be doing this, but if there's nobody helping you, how do you survive?'

And with that philosophical gem, Hugo ambled off, embarrassment written all over him. We carried on until we got to the bridge over the lake and stopped to watch the ducks.

'Quite envious of ducks.'

'Oh yes?'

'It's about lifestyle, I suppose. Think about it. All you've got to do is swim around looking decorative and people come up and feed you. Marvellous. And, if you're a bit short on the donated rations, all you've got to do is dabble for a bit. What's even better, is that some of them get to migrate. Just consider it . . . no more hot summers down here. As soon as you starts to get a bit warm, you says to your mates, "Come on, time to flap off to the Arctic for a bit of cool." Wonderful. Wish I could do the same. I hate the heat. You try wandering around in the summer dressed in a black overcoat.'

Hugo disconsolately kicked a pebble into the water, having first checked it wasn't edible. By unspoken agreement, we turned left to leave the park and walked into Kensington Gore.

'Royal Geographical Society, that is.' Hugo nodded towards a large red-brick building. 'Always wanted to go in there. Fascinated by exploration, guv. Should have been born a husky. Can't you see it: "Hugo of Labrador, the famous arctic explorer". Just think, there could have been a "Hugo Memorial Library and Exhibition" in there. Me mum would have been ever so proud.'

'What stopped you?'

'Usual story with an addict: addiction got in the way. I tell you what, though, there's an inner-wolf in all of us dogs, though you'd never believe it looking at a dachshund. I'm convinced it's what we dream about. You watch a dog asleep – properly asleep. He only does that when he's secure, otherwise there's always half an eye and an ear on watch. Well, when he's properly asleep, he's either dead to the world or he's dreaming. But you look at him when he's dreaming, it's always little woofs and paws twitching, as if he were running about. He never barks or snarls. I'm sure our dreams are always about being back in the wolf pack. Never had a bad dream in my life, guv. Even Arthur I only think about when I'm awake. All my dreams are about three things: food, snow and water. Might be something to do with being a Labrador, though. You watch next time you see a dog asleep.'

I wished I could agree, because I had seen Hugo asleep after he had told me about Arthur's accident. But on the whole I thought he was right: dogs' dreams seemed to be good ones. We carried on down Exhibition Road until we came to the Victoria and Albert Museum.

Hugo looked up. 'That's an art museum.'

'Never been in. Must go some day.'

'It reminds me . . .'

'Of what?'

'Of being in love. Ever been in love?'

'Certainly have.'

'I was once. Still am, I suppose. Never forgotten her anyway.'

'Who was she?'

'A standard white poodle. Name of Zoe. She was a Scouser, and pretty as a picture. Can't imagine what she saw in me. I was just a young "Jack the Lad" Labrador. She was gorgeous, worked as a life model at St Martin's School of Art. We spent a lot of time wandering about together. I used to think we were soul mates. She used to call me her bit of "ruff" – no pun intended, of course.'

'What happened to her?'

'I don't really know. I had a spot of bother with a chocolate cake I found and ended up in the animal hospital. I was an emergency. Took a long time to get better, and then they went and rehomed me. Well, that were a bit of a disaster. I know they took care to find a decent home, but I was still a young Lab and used to me freedom. I wasn't ready for the pipe-and-slippers bit and listening to conversations like, "Is he trained to the gun?" Me, trained to a gun? Can't abide the idea. The only retrieving I want to do is proper grub. Had to run away, and you've no idea how long it takes to get from Sunningdale to Soho if you don't know the way. By the time I got back, she'd disappeared. Love of my life she was, never got over it. She were the only dog that ever understood me.'

'It's all about consequences, you know. . .'

'I know. I really let myself go and everything got really out of hand. Stopped looking after myself and got terribly overweight. Everything went wrong after that. I got found out at the theatre. Dreadful row there was. Theatre manager came round late one night and found me. He weren't happy. "What's this fat, smelly dog doing in my theatre?" he said. Well, of course nobody owned up to knowing anything about me, they was all too worried about losing their jobs, so I was out on my ear with nowhere to sleep and a raging addiction problem.

'Trouble is, guv, when you're living on the edge stuff goes wrong easily. I thought I was sorted, roof over me head at night, regular breakfast, girlfriend, then the day round Soho and such and then back again. Look at me, one chocolate cake too many, rushed to the dog hospital, and the whole of me world collapses as a result. It was all me own fault, although it took me a long time to learn that.'

'What happened next?'

'My life became very chaotic. Started sleeping rough. That was scary. Mind you, had one advantage: being a black Lab, you're inconspicuous at night. You can merge into the shadows and people don't see you. Imagine what it would be like to be a Dulux dog? Try and curl up in a doorway and pretend you're not there and you get all sorts of grief. People go by and say, "Oh, look, isn't he cute, what's your name? Apple Blossom?" You could die of shame. Trouble is, you stand out like the proverbial. But that's just human eyes. Animals can smell you, even if they can't see you, and there are some really bad animals out there at night. They don't bother humans, but you imagine waking up and looking into the eyes of a gang of marauding mice. One of 'em I met was a real little blighter. Used to wait until I was asleep and then crawl quietly under an ear and whisper, "Food, chicken biryani, chow mein, gaucho steak . . ." Thought I was hearing voices until I found out. Couldn't sleep properly after that. Always had half an eye open and an ear cocked. Don't get much rest that way.'

'What did you do?'

'What any sensible dog would do: try and find a human. It was an old soldier who befriended me. Diamond bloke he was. It were a couple of months after I was kicked out of the theatre. Well, one day, after a good breakfast kindly donated by a stall holder in Berwick Street, I went on a bit of a stroll down towards Horseguards. Well, I'm having a sit down in front of the Guards Memorial, when this bloke comes up and pats me on the head. Upright he was, and neat, although his clothes were a bit shabby. "On your own, son?" he says. "Looking for company?"

'Well, truth be told,' said Hugo, 'it were just what I were looking for. I nuzzled into him and then rolled over and waved me paws in the air. He got the message. "Heel!" he said, and I promptly obliged, and off we marched back in the direction of Soho. Well, I wouldn't have Adam and Eve'd it, but he had a little flat near St Anne's Court off Wardour Street. Nice flat it were, and ever so clean and tidy. First thing he does is say, "You need a bath," and the next thing I know I'm in the tub being relieved of me "friends and relations" and six months of street grime. Five minutes in the suds and I came out a new Labrador. Then he says, "You need a collar." Well, I had a choke collar in Sunningdale, but I had managed to slip that off when I left. This were a proper leather one. I was terribly excited, felt like a proper cared-for dog. After that it were, "Now, Hugo, you're overweight and out of condition, so it's proper meals and regular exercise for you, my boy." I could see the logic in this, but I were a bit dubious it would work. You see, I'd been used to grazing when I wanted, the occasional complete blowout, and the odd period of hunger, but basically I was an eat-when-I-wanted sort of dog. The idea that I knew where my next meal was coming from was a good one, but I was a bit bothered about a lack of variety and a possible lack of in between meal snacks.'

'What about the exercise, Hugo?'

'That bothered me, too. Basically, I had always just bimbled around – kind of a metaphor for my life, really.'

'How did you get on?'

'Well, my old mum used to say to me, "Hugo, never, ever, look a gift horse in the mouth." I thought to myself . . . roof over head, regular meals, occasional bath, regular exercise, nice owner . . . what's not to like? Give it a whirl.'

By now we had reached South Kensington. We headed to Pret A Manger, where Hugo commandeered an outside space by sitting on a chair and putting his paws on the table. As there wasn't much of a queue inside I figured I could get us both lunch before management arrived to object.

'Fascinating place this, guv,' said Hugo as I returned with his favourite crayfish sandwich. 'Look at the people going by. They all have their heads down, looking at their mobile phones, or just in front of their feet to see where they are going. Nobody looks up to look around. They miss a lot that way.'

'Very observant of you.'

'Well, guv, when you've spent half your youth surviving on the streets you get to be savvy, checking everywhere out. Now, take Kensington, you gets the odd terraced restaurant, and the occasional bread roll falls down into the street from time to time. So, you looks up, sees a terrace and thinks, I'll just cross the road and check out beneath that. Once found some prawn vol au vents near here that had fallen over the railings from a party. Other thing is, if the restaurant is upstairs, there'll be bins somewhere, generally down near the fire escape at the rear, so it's worth a bit of a hunt.'

'You never cease to amaze me.'

'It goes further, guv. Once you starts looking up you see other stuff. You starts noticing the architecture. Take the Tube. Fascinating history, even has a tunnel to the museums. I like architecture, guv, at least the stuff before 1939. I reckon they've wrecked London since then. Don't agree with high-rise, spoils the skyline and makes you feel claustrophobic. You should see what they have done along the Thames.'

Hugo stared gloomily at the empty wrapper from his crayfish sandwich. Dribbles of saliva fell from his jowls on to the pavement. In a moment of madness, I got him another one. He looked at me with a mischievous grin. 'See, guv, I'm training you well.'

'Hugo,' I said, regretting my foolishness, 'training is the wrong word. "Manipulating" is closer to the mark.'

'Am I bovvered?' he said, through a mouthful of crayfish tails.

We got up and went to catch the bus home to Golders Green. Hugo stared out of the window, making the occasional disparaging remark about "Bloody high-rise glass and steel," and "Ruddy Romans fault for inventing concrete . . ." Clearly, for Hugo, Modernist and Brutalist were one and the same. Nothing could improve on the Classical order and brick, wood and stone. But, I reflected, it is hard to find a more traditional dog than a Labrador, even without the inner Arctic explorer.

Chapter 4

The Great Jermyn Street Cheese Heist

I had to go away and didn't see Hugo for a week. When I returned he was sitting on his bed looking thoughtful. As I went to say hello he shushed me and said, 'Give us ten minutes, guv, practising me mindfulness.'

I left him alone with his thoughts.

True to his word he reappeared on time.

'Hello, guv, how was France?'

'French, Hugo. How have you been?'

'Fair to muddling. Fancy a walk?'

'Of course. Did you have anywhere in mind?'

'Rather fancy going to Soho. Want to show you some of me old haunts.'

We took the Northern Line down to Tottenham Court Road and exited onto Oxford Street. Hugo led the way and soon turned down into Dean Street and stopped outside a famous curry restaurant.

'I'd love to go in there, guv, I've got a real thing about curry. Some of the best smells in London outside here. Must be amazing inside. I can just imagine it. Michelin-standard chicken biryani. Dog heaven.' He changed the subject. 'Fascinating place, Dean

Street, used to be home to the film industry, you know. I'd have loved to be a film star. I can see it now: "Hugo Labrador in 'The Call of the North,'" or "Hugo Labrador stars as the eponymous hero in Jack London's 'White Fang.'"

'Isn't that a part for a wolfdog, Hugo?'

'Don't like to say it, guv, but you have a bit of a tendency to rain on me parade sometimes.'

And with that parting shot Hugo put his head down and grumped his way down the road until we came to the turning for St Anne's Court.

'This is where I lived with the old soldier,' he said. 'It weren't a bad life, but it was also the beginning of me really serious problems.'

'How so?'

'Well, guv, to start with it were all good. I loved having a roof over me head, regular bath and meals and regular walks. But it were also a massive change. I'd been used to pleasing myself and I had a lot of variety in me grub. Now it were always the same: Obesity Management for dogs and the occasional Winalot and chew.'

'But that's pretty much how things are now, Hugo.'

'Begging your pardon, guv, that's not entirely true. I get to act as your sous chef and taste the odd morsel of your cooking, so I still gets some flavour and variety. Your pomodoro rustica and basil sauce goes down a treat, as you well know. Back then it was different. Very strict . . . fair but strict. Thing was, I began to yearn for me old life and I needed a real gut-busting meal on something tasty.'

'That must have been very worrying?'

'It was, guv, it was. I used to talk to his cat about it. Nice cat he were; bit strange-looking, though, on account of the fact that he was a cross between a ginger and an oriental. Had a head on his shoulders, too. "Hugo," he used to say, "you're feeling conflicted between what you want and what you ought to do. Need to sort your head out."

'Well, it was alright him saying that, sitting up straight, with his fur all groomed and his tail curled round him. Typical cat superiority. He should talk, though, he had this scam going: three separate people thought he was their cat, so three lots of treats. He'd let himself out of one flat, when they thought he'd gone to bed, and into the one over the corridor, and sit there purring whilst the owner tried to do his studying. When he didn't get enough attention, he used to sit on his laptop. That got his owner's attention, not always welcome either, because sometimes you'd hear this irritated meow as he got thrown off. Then he'd be round to the next place, where the bloke worked as a fish filleter at Billingsgate. He'd always get a late breakfast there out of scraps from the fish market. After that, he'd have a sleep somewhere and then come and find me for a chat. He'd got a good line in storytelling, too. He used to educate me about his great uncle, who was a man-eating tiger in Bengal. Fair hero-worshipped him he did. Can't see what's heroic about eating people myself, it would be too easy.'

'I'll ignore that last comment. What happened to you?'

'Well, I felt this pressure building up in me. There'd be voices in me head, one saying, "Go on, Hugo, just a short escape and a rummage in the bins behind a Chinese in Gerard Street!"; but the other voice would say, "You mustn't, Hugo, listen to the cat's advice, sort your head out and stay safe." Terrible it was. But gradually the need for a forage won out.

'I bided me time until the old soldier was just about to fasten me lead to me collar, and I bolted. I heard him calling after me, but I just ran until he was out of sight. Soon as I could I started exploring the bins behind the restaurants. Didn't take long to strike lucky, and I just ate and ate until I couldn't manage any more. Then I stopped for a few minutes to let it go down, and then started again. That done it really. As soon as I had me blowout I felt ashamed, but I felt I couldn't go back because I'd let the old soldier down. Back on the streets I were. Thrown everything away just because I couldn't control me appetite. Same as before when I lost Zoe. I thought, can't hang around Soho, I'm too well known here. After a bit of thought I remembered Borough Market, getting closer to where I grew up by the biscuit factory. Plenty of food available in the market. So, off I went. Down to Waterloo Bridge, over the river and a sharp turn left, and headed off in the general direction of the Globe Theatre. I felt good. Back roaming and a general license to scrump.'

'Didn't you feel sorry about the old soldier?'

'A little bit. But the thing is, when you're in the grip of your food drive, the only thing that matters is grub. Anyway, there I am in the Borough, back doing me old thing, roaming about, sleeping rough and eating everything I can lay me paws on. Only this time it's different. First time since me mum died I had experienced love and affection – apart from with Zoe, that was – and knew what it was like to have a roof over your head and a sort of family around you. And now I'd gone and chucked it away. Result is, I'm not some Jack the Lad Labrador with a swagger and a taste for fine dining, but a miserable, soon to be middle-aged Labrador, who is homeless, ownerless and partnerless. So, what happens? How do I resolve me problems? I eat more, and start to get seriously fat and scruffy. Hugo, I'd say to myself, this not a good idea; yet off I'd go on the hunt for a dropped hamburger. Genius.'

'It's the same with all addicts, Hugo.'

'I know now, guv, but actually knowing that doesn't make it any better. You go into this limbo period, where you know what you're doing is bad for you but you pretends it isn't, and you denies it to anybody who tries to tell you. Anyway, the months go by, I'm even more overweight and scruffy, and with quite a lot of "friends and relations", if you get me drift. I'm sitting under the railway arches dozing off, when suddenly, wham! I'm trapped in a big net. Look up and it's some bloke from the council who has caught me. "Been after you for a while, mate," he says. "Had reports about you." He and his assistant put me in the van and, next thing I know, I'm back in the animal hospital. "Hello," they say. "Hugo, again. Would sir like his normal room, or perhaps sir would prefer our guest suite with a sea view?" Well, I tell you, guv, I'm not great on sarcasm, so I gave 'em my best withering look. Mark you, it was my first experience of compassion fatigue in a care worker, not that I recognised it then. After that they have a look at me collar and, bless his heart, but the old soldier had put his telephone number on it. Changed their tune after that. "We must call him," they said, "and clean you up."'

We walked on through St Anne's Court, past the Good Housekeeping Institute.

'Wasn't easy living here with all the food about. Used to be a little café in the corner.' Hugo pointed to a boarded shop front. 'It were Ecuadorean, always smelt wonderful when I went by. What's escabeche, guv?'

'It's a way of cooking, Hugo. Basically, the food is "'cooked" in vinegar or citrus juice. In Ecuador they do a very good prawn escabeche, and you could probably do it with crayfish tails.'

'Doesn't sound very filling, guv.'

'It isn't intended to be; it's supposed to be clean-tasting and flavoursome and very light. It's very good.'

'I think I'll stick to biryani.'

'A wise choice, Hugo.'

'Thing is, guv, I know I'm a food addict, and always will be. I know how to manage to keep it under control, I just struggle with doing what I know I am supposed to. I'm not overweight or anything at the moment, and I can hold me job down as a therapist Labrador, but I don't feel good about myself. I can still see other dogs looking at me down their noses and saying to themselves, "We can master our appetites until the next meal; just look at him." Hurtful I find it, guv, really hurtful.'

I had learnt that there was a very sensitive side to Hugo. He generally kept it hidden under an air of bravado, but he had been scarred by his life experiences, for all that he made light of them. He was a thoughtful dog, and in all the time we had been together I rarely heard him utter an unkind word about anybody. He treated everybody as a friend and hoped to be treated in the same way.

Hugo stopped as we came out into Wardour Street.

'Used to find it a great trial when I walked through here. See the chocolate shop over the road? I would have died to get in there. I used to press my nose up against the window and read the labels. Can you believe it, guv, salted caramel chocolate brownies with cocoa nib. Now that really is Labrador heaven.'

'But dangerous, Hugo. A bit like eating fugu: you never know if you might die.'

'Had a close-run thing near here.'

'Want to tell me about it?'

'Well, after the old soldier collected me from the animal hospital we had a bit of a talk. "Hugo, my boy," says he, "you've got to get a bit of discipline in your life. Got to be steady in the face of fire – or, in your case, chicken biryani." He was right, of course, but it doesn't help. You can tell an addict until you are blue in the face to stop eating. All that happens is that the words fill your head with images of food you're not going to be allowed to eat if they have their way.'

'So, what happened?'

'Well, I went back home with him, and it was back to square one again: regular meals, regular exercise, bed put neat and tidy every morning after I got up – "kit inspection" he called it. No doubt he loved me, though. Trouble was that it was love with organisation, and I wasn't ready for it. I used to have long chats with his cat about it; but he kept on going on about getting me head sorted out. "Hugo," he would say, "you're no use to anybody like this. You should be giving back some of that famed Labrador love and devotion, not mooching about the flat, on the scrounge for leftovers. "However," he said, "they do say there's no help for an addict until they reach rock-bottom."

'Well, guv, that got me worried. It had been pretty tough until then. I thought, it's got to get worse before I stand a chance of getting better? Couldn't imagine that. What else could go wrong? I could see the odd blowout requiring a trip to the animal hospital, but I could cope with that. Suppose I'd never really thought about what was required to get control of me eating.'

'So, what happened near here?'

'Gone for a walk with the old soldier. Usual trip down through St James's Park and across to the Guards Memorial, then up the steps into Pall Mall and on up towards the place we've decided to call the "Scottish Line", guv. Anyway, this time–'

'I can guess, Hugo, you turned left into Jermyn Street and went to the cheese shop.'

'How do you know?'

'I used to do that exact walk with my grandfather. When I was a little boy I spent my school holidays with my grandparents. Grandfather used to take me to feed the ducks. Grandma used to give us a bag of stale bread for them.'

'Wouldn't have lasted the walk to the ducks if you had me with you,' said Hugo. 'You do know it's bad for them?'

'I do now, Hugo. Then we would walk on to the cheese shop in Jermyn Street. It was a place of wonderment for me, then, with scrubbed floorboards and sawdust on the floor and whole cheeses stacked up. There were sides of bacon hanging from the ceiling.'

'Guv, stop. You're raising me demons.'

'Oh, sorry, Hugo, I got a bit carried away. Very fond of my grandfather, I was, lots of very happy memories.'

'That's as maybe, but I need to stay on the straight and narrow, so if you've done with your reminiscing about foody grandparents I would be grateful.'

I had forgotten how brittle addicts could be, and how so often conversations like this were like walking on egg shells.

'Self-same cheese shop,' said Hugo. 'Never been in one before and, after chocolate, next best thing to Labrador heaven. Of course he'd left me outside. Usual trick: "Sit, stay," with a reward of half a Bonio. I ask you, guv, food addict parked outside one of the best cheese shops in London and your owner thinks "Sit, stay" and a bit of a Bonio is all that's needed.

'Well, in he goes and I gets the waft of cheese as he opens the door. Now, you remember the smell of that shop from when you were a kid, so imagine me, nose that's a thousand times more sensitive than yours. Out comes Brie de Meaux, Camembert, Dolcellatte, Parmesan . . . oh, guv, the Parmesan, shaving it they were. I could see little fresh shavings of Parmesan going onto greaseproof paper. The smell. It was the agony and the ecstasy all rolled into one.

'Well, that done it. Next bloke that opens the door I'm straight in with him. Blow half a Bonio to sit nonsense. I grabs the first cheese to hand and makes for the door in the commotion. You should have heard the racket. Anyway, I manages to get out and make a run for it. Didn't have time to eat, and I was off with me lead flying behind me and me jaws firmly clamped round what turned out to be a half a Peccorino. Good job it was a really hard cheese, couldn't have made it with a Gorgonzola, would only have been left with a mouthful, and I'd have been caught trying to pick up the bits I dropped.

'I go flying through St James's Square and make it down to his self-same park. I find a big enough bush to hide under and settle down to enjoy me lunch. Very tasty it were, and I savoured every morsel. I was just thinking about popping down to the lake for a quick drink, when a park attendant grabs hold of the end of me lead saying, "And what 'ave we 'ere?" Nearly jumped out of me skin, I did, thought I was safely hidden. I'd forgotten about the lead. Fortunately, he was so surprised by me sudden movement he drops the lead and I was off again. Only this time I'm starting to feel a bit wobbly, on account of all the cheese I've just eaten, and I'm developing this raging thirst. Long story short, I end up on the Embankment, down near where they've got a statue to good Queen Boadicea – prefer that name personally, guv, don't hold with calling her Boodica.

'I pops down to the landing stage to have a drink out of the river. Next thing I know there's a bump as a riverboat docks and, because I'm still feeling wobbly, I'm off me paws and into the wet stuff. Weren't very funny, either. I was still terribly thirsty, not feeling at all special, and me paws wouldn't work properly. I tried to swim, but the river was on the full ebb and I got swept away. Then me lead got caught on something and I went under.'

Chapter 5

The Dogs Home

"'Tower Lifeboat, Tower Lifeboat, Thames Coastguard, Thames Coastguard. . .'" Channel zero crackled to life on the RNLI's E-Class lifeboat. "'Thames Coastguard, Tower Lifeboat." " Report of a dog in the water by Westminster Pier. Should be coming your way, if It's still afloat.'"

And with that exchange over, Hugo's rescue swung into action. The crew of the Tower Lifeboat, which had been about to dock, eased the boat back into the strongly ebbing tide and started under Waterloo Bridge. They scanned the water, knowing that there was only a slight chance that the dog hadn't already been swept past them.

Hugo took up the story.

'Thought me time was up; but then, all of a sudden, whatever had held me down freed, and I bobbed to the surface – great improvement on being under all that brown stuff. Next thing I knows, there's this orange boat by the side of me and a hand comes down, grabs me by the collar, takes me round the back of the boat, and hauls me aboard. Was I grateful? But I was none too special after a big dose of river water on top of half a Peccorino. Fair disgraced myself in the boat I did. But the crew were very good about it. Brought me back to the lifeboat station, washed me off and hosed the boat down. Had a good rub down with a towel and I sat all forlorn in the crew room. Next thing there's a bowl of clean water and somebody produces some Winalot. Very gentlemanly of them, I thought. Then they have a look at me collar and make a few phone calls.

'I sat in the crew room for quite a time. They were all very nice to me – dog-friendly I would say. Got lots of pats and Winalot. I thought with a bit of luck they might adopt me, and I could become station dog, but it didn't happen because the old soldier had pitched up. They had got his telephone number off me collar. The old soldier looks all serious at me. "Hugo, my boy," he says, "this can't go on. I love you dearly, but you are too much of a handful for me. I'm taking you to the dogs home where they can look after you and try and find you a new home." I was devastated, because I'd been here before. Me own fault again, and now there was going to be even more hassle and grief cooped up in the dogs home, wondering when, or if, I would ever get out.'

Hugo sighed.

'His cat had talked to me about food bingeing and the consequences, but I just couldn't seem to get the hang of controlling my urges. Anyway, the old soldier took a firm hand on me lead and, after thanking everybody profusely for their trouble, takes me off. Well, we have a bit of a march and we end up at a dogs home. Very smart and comfortable it was, but it was still a dogs home without any food opportunities other than what you were given. Felt a bit like being in prison. I expected someone to come along with a set of pyjamas for me, covered in arrows. Anyway, clang! and I'm in a cell with a bowl of water and a bed and not a sight of a restaurant dustbin anywhere. I felt really miserable. None of me mates, still a bit wobbly from me adventures and, to use a hackneyed phrase "dog-tired".'

"You really did have a talent for snatching "defeat from the jaws of victory", Hugo.'

'Tell me about it, guv. After a bit, everything settled down to a routine. Had a vet inspection, got enough jabs to join the army, and then it was regular meals and regular exercise in the prison yard. Rest of the time you spent sleeping or talking to your cellmate. Occasionally, some fresh faces would appear and you'd hear, "Look, Mummy, a nice Labrador," and then you'd hear whispering, and some grown up would say, "Not that one, darling, he's got a reputation for being a terrible handful."

'Well, I got really upset over that and I'd go back to me bed all morose and have another kip. Sometimes, just to add insult to injury, they'd choose your cellmate, and then you'd be on your own for a bit until they found another companion for you. After a while, I began to think I was jinxed, and you could hear the other dogs whispering, "That's the black Lab with a problem."'

Hugo looked thoughtful.

'I had a lot of time to think about things. The weeks turned into months and I went into the "Difficult to Rehome" program. First Labrador ever, they said. I took it really hard, guv. You know me, I'm a kindly soul, never wished anybody any harm, just got a bit of a problem with food. Thing is, somehow my record at the animal hospital caught up with me. That meant that anybody taking me on knew they was taking on a handful.

'Anyway, when they put you on the program they move you to another part of the dogs home, so you was with other dogs they were also having difficulty with. Sort of "old lag's wing". Then we had sessions with a dog psychologist. I found these really interesting. Never really thought about me problems in such detail. We also had group therapy, where us dogs hung out together and talked about our issues. I thought it were a bit of a joke to start with, as all we did at the beginning was compare notes on the best way to break into a dustbin, stake out a family picnic, or keep a lookout for trouble. We weren't all food addicts, of course. Some were really wayward, and a bit handy with their teeth and paws you might say. They had some special sessions for dealing with their violence issues, but we all got on pretty well, kind of partners in adversity, as it were.

'Now, my problem was that I knew I had problems, knew I was an addict, and knew I caused trouble. Didn't mind admitting it. But until I went into the dogs home didn't much want to do anything about it. I'd lived by me wits, had a few close shaves, always got off with me winning smile and personality, and was quite happy with me lot. Didn't want to change and didn't know how to change neither. Looking back, I had turned into me dad, only less handy with me paws.

'One day, we went to one of our therapy sessions, and there was this pit bull. Pretty battle-hardened he looked too, covered in scars. Looked a bit like an old marine sergeant. Anyway, he were the calmest dog I'd ever met. Had this serenity about him. Never come across it before. Turned out he lived at the dogs home and they put him into our therapy sessions as a sort of role model, to help guide us. He used to talk to us about manners and behaviour. Made me feel quite ashamed, as I'd given up practising most of what me mum had taught me.

'I asked this pit bull what had happened to him, because it looked like he had been pretty handy with the aggravation in the past. "Hugo," he said to me, "I was a really bad dog and nearly ended up being put down on account of it. I ended up in here, on a compulsory therapy program: mend your ways, or else. I had to take it seriously. But the funny thing was that I was helped most by one of the young volunteer humans. He was a bit of a hippy, not like the skinhead that had owned me before. I'd never met a gentle human being. I'd been trained to snarl and attack, and here was this bloke who'd just sit there quietly and talk to me. Mark you, he weren't stupid, he left me muzzle on for weeks until he were quite sure I'd calmed down. One day he said to me, 'Do you know, some people believe dogs are going to be reincarnated as humans in their next life?' That was a bit complex for me. I'd had enough trouble coping with this life without thinking about the next. Well, he gradually introduces me to the idea that life always has its ups and downs, and how much of a problem that is depends on how you look at it. 'Reggie,' he would say to me, 'you need a philosophy of life.' You can imagine what it was like telling a pit bull he needed a philosophy of life; bit like telling him to get religion. Anyone told you to get religion, Hugo?"

'Looked at them once, Reggie, I said to him They all seemed to involve fasting; couldn't cope with that. Mind you, there's a synagogue I know where they seem to have good parties. There's normally a smoked salmon bagel or two going round the back when the proceedings are all over. And

I thought about Buddhism when I heard they practised the "middle way": no fasting and no excess. Thought that might be me way out of me food addiction. They seemed pretty handy with the begging bowl too, and I'd mastered that a long time ago. But you know what it's like as a street dog . . . too busy surviving to give any attention to anything other than survival.'

'"That's just it," Reggie had said, "to make any progress you've got to get beyond just surviving. Now, in your case, Hugo, your life is dominated by food. It is more important to you than your friends and family. That's why you ended up in here. The old soldier couldn't cope with you any more, although he loved you dearly. You can't even find a family to take you because of your reputation."

'I knew Reggie was right. Trouble was, that although I knew he was right, I still couldn't quite bring myself to cut back on my eating. I still had that feeling that said, "Tell you what, one last mega-binge and that will be it; one last chicken biryani for four as a takeout, and I'll give it up for good."

'Reggie looked at me and shook his head. "It won't do, Hugo. You 'ave to mend your ways. The trouble is, that I know you won't until you reach rock-bottom. But it's a race as to whether food kills you first." I looked at him disconsolately. You know, Reggie, I said to him, being in here doesn't help. The food is boring, there is not enough of it, and there's no flavour. Apart from sitting around talking and the odd walk there's nothing to do. I'm bored, and when I'm bored all I do is think about food. "Hugo," Reggie said, "you're giving in and making excuses. You have got to start thinking about why you are here and your life. You are getting lots of help, but all you are doing is playing Jack the Lad. Time to grow up." And with that Reggie turned his back on me and carried on with the other dogs in the session.

'I tell you, guv, he really rocked me back. Made me finally start to think about myself. Normally, I just bounced along. Foraging, engaging with people who I thought might offer me food, and ignoring those who didn't. I'd already been told that all I did was use people and other dogs, and that proper relationships involved putting in at least as much as you took out. This had never been my style, ever since I had left home; and for some time before that, life had been a struggle. I suppose that it had all started with me dad. He was great to be around, and he tried to help, but he didn't really know much, not about life, only about surviving. He wasn't a role model. It was Dad who showed us how to forage, and he encouraged the devil-may-care attitude to life that got me into so much trouble.'

Hugo broke off and stared at the ground.

'I tell you, guv, I was not a happy Labrador. I went back to me "cell", lay down on me mat and had a long hard sulk.'

'What happened next, Hugo?'

'Not a lot really. Carried on with the same old routine. Went through the motions of going to me classes and watched cellmates come and go. It all got very boring and I got very miserable. Sleep wasn't any help. I'd lay on me bed with that look that says, "eyes open but rest of me out to lunch", and daydream about being rescued and everything being OK again, and then, at night-time, when I properly closed my eyes, I'd get these troublesome dreams about me family and food.'

'I thought you said dogs always had happy dreams?'

'I were just kidding you, guv. Anyway, one day Reggie says, "Hugo, there's someone I would like you to meet." Well,

I says, oh yeah, who might that be? Another dog-shrink? Reggie just looked at me in that calm, thoughtful way of his. "We have been really worried about you, Hugo. Nothing seems to be working. You just lie about getting more morose and spending all your time thinking about the past. We are going to move you to a new home, far out in the country, where you are going to have lots of fresh air and exercise and a new pack of dogs to socialise with."

'Guv, I just looked at him. I'm a Londoner, I said. Apart from one unsuccessful rehoming in Sunningdale, I've rarely strayed more than ten miles west of Bermondsey. How will I survive? I don't even speak the lingo? "Don't worry, Hugo," Reggie said, "they still speak English, just with a different accent, you will be fine."

'Well, I thought, can't be worse than staying here, and so that was it. They packed me blanket and bowl in a small grip, together with some emergency rations, in case of breakdowns, and loaded me up in a white van – you know, one of those with a little fan on the roof to keep you cool. I said to them as they was loading me – couldn't have found a proper soft top, could you? I fancy arriving in style. "Not a chance, Hugo," they said, "can't take a chance of you hopping it at a motorway service station." Didn't know what a motorway service station was and, I have to say, when I did, I didn't think much of 'em. Anyway, slam goes the door and we're off.

'Now, although I'm a metropolitan dog, I am always up for new experiences and, anyway, I'd been cooped up in the dogs home for far too long. Mark you, it was all a bit puzzling. I got to notice these road signs and I asked the driver why Hampshire was so named. He hadn't a clue. But his passenger, who was one of the dog psychologists, who'd come along with me for the ride, helped out. He was an interesting bloke, very clever and knowledgeable. Learnt a lot from him I did. He explained that Hampshire wasn't just a place for posh picnics, and that "hamp" was not a contraction of "hamper".

'It got worse when we got to Wiltshire. I couldn't get me head around the idea that a very long time ago somebody called Wilt had a small settlement here. Why Wilt? I asked, there must have been lots of other people? Problem was, when I saw Wilt I thought of vegetables, lettuce and such like, very tasty too. Mark you, Wiltshire got worse. Where did this Moonraker story come from? Why would you hide something consumable in a pond and then try and fish it out under a full moon with a rake?

'Made me realise what a gulf there is between town and country, guv. Somerset was easier – there wasn't a food connection in the name, and I could understand naming the place after summer fields. But then we came to Devon. Why would you want to name it after some ancient tribe who were here with the Romans? Dumnonii, I ask you. Doesn't even sound like Devon? No good came of the Romans, they gave the world concrete, and you know what I think about that.

Then I see this sign for Cornwall. I'd heard of Cornwall. The folks I had temporary lodgings with in Sunningdale were always banging on about Cornwall – "Got a little country cottage at Daymer Bay, darling, don't you know." Well, I didn't, and I didn't hang around neither. I always thought it must be an interesting place, though, being named after walls of corn. I got overtones of Shredded Wheat in my head. You know, with hot milk and brown sugar. Fair salivating, if not outright drooling, at the thought. Then this psychologist bloke tells me that the first syllable might represent a tribe, the Cornovii, and the second comes from the old English for a foreigner. Didn't believe him, though, and continued to think of it as Shredded Wheatshire. Cornwall, really . . .'

Hugo stopped. We had been so immersed in his reminiscences that we had been walking without taking in where we were. We had left Wardour Street long behind us and found ourselves in Chandos Place, just at the entrance to Maiden Lane.

'You seem to be in familiar territory,' Hugo said to me.

'Certainly am, Hugo, went to medical school here, and my dad used to take me to lunch in Rules when he came to London.'

'Beef was good in there; trouble was, it was too good and there was never much by way of leftovers. Much better pickings in Soho.'

'Going back to your Cornwall trip, how did you get on with the place names?'

'The dog psychologist explained that there was a Cornish language and there was this phrase, "By Tre, Pol and Pen shall ye know Cornishmen," but it didn't really make any sense to me. Lot of things didn't make sense in Cornwall, at least not at first.'

We entered into Southampton Street and crossed Covent Garden to the Opera House.

'Ever been in there?'

'Not for a long time, Hugo. Slept on the streets once to get a ticket for Fonteyn and Nureyev dancing in "Swan Lake".'

'Blimey, guv, you are old, that was ages ago! Don't go much for ballet. Not really a medium for Labradors.'

'Or other dogs, Hugo.'

'I dunno, guv, might be OK for poodles.'

And with that Hugo sniffed, his tail dropped, and I knew he was thinking about his lost girlfriend.

'Used to come up here early in the morning with Zoe, when the market was still here. The pubs used to open early for the stall holders, so there used to be early pickings to be had. Found a full English breakfast once, dropped on the pavement. Guv, I'm hungry, couldn't stand me a pizza, could you? It's been a long and emotional day.'

'Of course I can, Hugo. Mum's the word, though, or I will get in terrible trouble with your mistress.'

'OK, but you'd better lay off the garlic oil on mine, or she'll know for certain.'

An hour later and we ambled down to Trafalgar Square, found a place to sit and fell asleep in the sun.

Sometime later: 'Guv?'

'Yes, Hugo?'

'I've had enough for today. Can we go home?'

'Of course, but I am really keen to hear more of your story.'

'I've reached the end of the beginning, if you like, but it's all been a bit much today and I could do with a rest.'

We found a bus and went home.

Chapter 6

The Blue Lobster

It would be several weeks before Hugo and I had another day out. I had to visit an old patient, who was having a tough time. He lived near Aldeburgh and I thought Hugo might like to come along for the ride.

'Now you're talking, fresh sea air, bit of seagull-mithering, crab to eat, crash of the surf, more crab, fish 'n chips for lunch. Couldn't be better.'

He sat in the back seat of the car, with the rear window open enough to get the passing smells.

'Don't know how you manage,' came from the back seat.

'What's up?'

'Everything goes by so quickly. I was just thinking that must be McDonald's when the next thing I get is hay being turned. All very confusing. Interesting, but confusing. No time to savour and reminisce. You know this place where we're going?'

'Quite well. Used to be taken there as a boy. Once I went there in the winter and they had a circus staying. Took a picture of an elephant on the seafront with my Box Brownie.'

'Quite the happy snapper. Think I'll have a sleep.'

We drove on in silence. Arriving at my patient's house I debated whether to leave Hugo in the car.

'It's alright, guv,' said Hugo, 'he's dog-friendly and I won't talk.'

'How do you know he's dog-friendly?'

'I can smell.'

'But he hasn't opened the door yet?'

'He doesn't need to, I can smell.'

Sure enough, we were both welcomed in.

'Does your dog want some water, there's a bowl in the kitchen?'

I caught Hugo's look. A silent, why do nice humans always offer water? I like water, but only to wash food down or on a scorching day. The polite thing in a dog world would be to say, would you like to clean my breakfast plate, didn't leave much I'm afraid, but there is the residue of some good Suffolk eggs and bacon and, with that, etiquette would be satisfied. But a bowl of water . . . He stomped over to the other side of the room, lay down and adopted his don't bother me, I'm out to lunch expression.

We left about an hour later. True to his word, there hadn't been a peep out of him.

When we were safely back in the car and on our way to the beach, he piped up, 'Don't think you need me.'

''Why is that, Hugo?'

'You did pretty well in there; better than I thought you would. Interesting.'

'What struck you most?'

'Oh, it's the trauma thing. Poor bloke, minding his business doing an ordinary job, nobody notices him; then suddenly he's caught up in a tragedy just outside his office window. Being a good Samaritan, he goes to help before the cavalry arrives. Then it's all blues and twos, and he quietly goes back to doing what he was doing before the accident – and nobody notices he was ever there. But he was there, and he's seen stuff that nobody should see.'

'I know, Hugo, and it gets worse. Because he's just a little guy quietly doing his job, he's not good at speaking up for himself and, as you heard, he got very depressed and nearly lost his job. Nobody, not even he, saw the link between the accident and his suffering. I thought we had got him cured a few years ago, but his son had a near-miss in a car and it brought everything back to him. We'll get him a bit more help and he'll be fine again, at least for a while.'

We parked the car on the seafront, some way along the road to Thorpeness. We walked up onto the beach.

'You didn't tell me it was gravel and stone, guv,' said Hugo, accusingly. 'Terribly hard work this is.'

'It's called shingle. Put up with it, Hugo, you get to choose your crab soon.'

Hugo cheered up. His nose had already caught the distant smells from the tarred wooden shacks on the beach, and he could see the fishing boats hauled up in the distance. Beyond that the RNLI lifeboat house loomed.

'That what I think it is?'

'Yes, it's the Aldeburgh branch of the folk that hauled you out of the Thames. Bigger boat, though. They're very Labrador-friendly there. We will drop in sometime and you might get to meet Station Dog George. He's a black Lab like yourself. Bit younger and thinner, though.'

'I shall ignore that.'

We walked on, the shingle scrunching under our feet.

'It's really hard work this. Three paws forward and one paw back, as you might say.'

'It will help you work up an appetite, Hugo.'

I got a hard stare. 'Come on, guv, you know me better than that. Since when has lack of an appetite been a problem?'

Arriving at the fish huts, Hugo started an inspection. 'Them lobsters, guv?'

'Absolutely.'

'One of them's bright blue, why is that?'

'Genetic mutation, Hugo.'

'Do they taste different?'

'No.'

'Can I 'ave one?'

'No.'

'Why not?'

'I haven't had any advances on your book yet. I promise you a bright blue lobster when I have. They still turn red when cooked, though. Oh, I forgot, you can't see red, can you?'

Hugo grunted. 'Bloody commerce, gets in the way of everything.'

We settled for a large pot of crab meat and went in search of a bakery. Later, rolls in hand, we sat down on a bench in the sun and consumed our fare.

Hugo was a crab connoisseur. 'I like this, guv, but it's a lot of hard work for only a little bit of food. These local crabs is only two mouthfuls. Now, if you could find a king crab?'

'It'll have to do for now, Hugo. You were telling me a while back about your trip to Cornwall. You described your journey down as sort of "the end of the beginning".'

Hugo looked up at me. 'It's quite a long story and I'm

very comfortable sitting here looking at the waves. Not in a hurry, are you?'

'No, Hugo. Plenty of time. We can sit here until high tide and then we have to go.'

'Hmmm,' went Hugo, 'well at least we're far enough up the beach for you not to need to do a King Canute.'

'Can we get on with the story?'

'Everything started changing after that journey. Eventually, we turn off the road through some great big gates and go down a very long drive into a valley. There's a big house, built out of granite, and a garden that went on forever. I saw a few humans around, some of 'em wearing funny robes, before they whisked me round the back to my new quarters. Well, the quarters. You should have seen 'em. You know the usual sort: run about a metre and a half wide so that someone can get in with a shovel for you know what, chain link fencing and a bit of shelter, and a few towels for a bed. Not a bit of it here. There was a proper area to do your business, nice tiles instead of concrete, a little summerhouse for privacy specially equipped with this lovely memory foam bed with sides to keep out the draft. Not that there was any. Proper Priory Hospital for dogs it were.

'I settled in very nicely, thank you. I was a bit concerned when they brought me me first bowl of food, though, because it were all vegetarian. I thought, what's up here, no shin of beef, no pork knuckle? But I have to admit it were very tasty. A lot more variety than just Obesity Management for dogs if I may say so.

'They left me to settle in. I met the other dogs and got used to the layout of the grounds. There was a beautiful garden that followed a stream down to the sea. It opened onto a small beach, and you could have a dip in the waves and then clean the salt off your coat in the stream. Perfect. It was all very secluded. No sign of any other road or path out, and definitely nowhere for any food opportunities. There was a kitchen garden, but that was walled and always out of bounds to us dogs. At the side of the beach there was a big open-sided hut that I found out later they used as a classroom for us.

'It all really started on day three. I was laying on me memory foam mattress, trying to work out what it was supposed to remember, when this nice girl comes along and says, "Come along, Hugo, time for your class." Class, what class? said I. I'm too old for school and I didn't have any education, anyway. "You're starting your twelve-paws program, Hugo. It's for dogs with food addiction." Fat chance of curing that, I told her. People have tried everything. The old soldier I lived with once put mustard, chilli powder and Worcester sauce around the lid of his food bin. Didn't make any difference, improved the taste if anything. Still ate the bin contents and licked the bin lid clean. Just had a bit of trouble with me business the next day, if you'll pardon me saying so. "Oh, we aren't going to do anything like mustard and chilli, Hugo. We're going to help you gain some control. You'll see." Little does she know, I thought. But seeing as how I didn't seem to have a choice in the matter I went along with her.

'She takes me down to the beach hut and I meet up with a bunch of other dogs. We have a bit of a chat, and it seems that we're all there for the same thing: food addiction. Well, it won't come as a surprise to you that most of us were Labs and retrievers – although there was a beagle and a dachshund. Poor little bloke, he had eaten so much he could barely get his belly off the ground. Nothing against 'em, but it really is a daft shape for a dog. He told me that dachshunds had been bred to go down badger holes. I said to him, size you are, mate, you'd be better off going down something bigger – more like a mineshaft. He were a bit offended at that. "Look in a mirror," he said. He were right, though. There was a mirror in my quarters, and I have to say every time I caught a glimpse of myself I had to look away.

'Anyway, we all gets called to order by the girl who brought me down and are given a treat each for sitting in an orderly row. Two things come into me head. First was, I like this place, I'll go to talks if they give us treats. Then I thought, if we are a bit more disorderly, will we get more treats when we behave again? That's always the flaw in reward-based training, guv. Got to be very clear you aren't rewarding bad behaviour.

'Then our lecturer comes in. He welcomes us and tells us a bit about where we are staying. It was a retreat and therapy place for humans and dogs, and strongly Buddhist-based, hence the people in yellow robes wandering around, and specialised in dogs with really serious food addiction. First thing he says is that food addiction is really difficult to deal with. Well, I didn't need telling that, I whispered to the dachshund. Only trouble was, he was so far beneath me I had to speak up a bit and I got heard. Lecturer looks at me. "Hugo . . ." he says, "it is Hugo, isn't it?" Yes, your worship, says I. "One more out-of-order comment and you get to come up and sit on the naughty step facing the class." This titter goes round the class and they chorused, "And you won't get any more treats today!" I felt a right idiot. Wasn't any point in blushing, though. Doesn't show when you're a black Lab. I just sat there with a stupid grin on me face.

'After that the lecturer starts up again. "As I was saying," he says, "food addiction is difficult to deal with. With most addictions you have a simple choice: you either stop taking whatever you are addicted to or you don't. The problem is, recognising that you are an addict and then deciding, more than anything else in the world, that you want to deal with it. If you are a food addict it's different, as you have to learn how to control your addiction, because you are addicted to something you also need. Now, Hugo, you were ready with helpful comments just now, are there any foods you are particularly addicted to?"

'I've got some really bad ones, I told him. Steak and chicken biryani. And anything with tomato and basil sauce, with parmesan. Trouble is, I also can't resist chocolate cake, even though I know how dangerous it is.

'"Umm," he goes, "how about you, Duchess?" turning to a more-than-overweight beagle, two down from me. "Anything, really," simpered Duchess. "Though I'm particularly partial to pasta." He went on, round us dogs, same question, similar answers. He came back to me. "Any others, Hugo?" Well, there's cheese, chips and chorizo, I said. "Hugo, you're having me on," said the lecturer. I'm not, boss, I promise, I told him. I just have this thing with spelling. All sorts of words remind me of food. There are lots of foods I like that start with "ch", and I have to avoid places that start with ch as well. Never go near Charing Cross, for example, or Chipping Camden, or Chipping Sodbury, or even Chepstow for that matter. "Hugo, that's fascinating. Quite remarkable. Now then, all of you, we are going to start you on our twelve-paws program. It is modelled on the twelve-steps program for people with addictions. Have any of you heard of this?"

'One dog wagged his tail,' said Hugo. 'Turned out he used to be owned by a publican who liked his tipple. The rest of us just sat there wondering what was coming next. Well, it seems that the first step is accepting you've got a problem, that you are powerless over your food drive, and that your life is unmanageable. I had no problem with that; you don't end up as a regular visitor to the animal hospital and being hauled out of the river by the RNLI without realising you've got something wrong in the existing department.

'Turns out that some of the dogs didn't think the same way, as they could recognise the problem in everybody else but not in themselves. Quite an argument ensued. It was interesting looking at it from the outside. The dogs that seemed to have the biggest problem with recognising their addiction were the ones who were fed too much by their owners. Seems their owners were also overweight, so the dog and his human validated each other. Our prof – that's what I had taken to calling our lecturer – said what had happened was that their owners had become co-dependent. Funny thing was, you know how dogs get to look like their owners?'

'You know, Hugo, we say that phrase the other way round.'

'Guv, sometimes you're very dim. Of course you would,' came Hugo's response. 'As I was saying, before being so rudely interrupted, you know how dogs look like their owners? Well, the funny thing is that the owners got to look as "cuddly", you might say, as their dogs. Made you wonder who had the addiction? Prof said the dogs not believing they were addicts was a form of "cognitive dissonance". Sort of getting very uncomfortable when you are told something that conflicts with your beliefs. Fortunately, I've always recognised I was a food addict. I've always tried to see things for what they actually are. Haven't always taken any notice, but I've at least tried.

'Well, after that little shindig we was dismissed and told we could go and play about on the beach for half an hour. You should have seen it. Couple of bunches of dogs, each the size of a butter mountain, sitting on the beach arguing that they were slim, really, or maybe just a tiny bit cuddly. I took myself off for a walk and went and looked in the rock pools. Ever seen a hermit crab, guv?'

'Yes, I used to watch them in the rock pools on the north Cornish coast when I was a boy. Fascinating.'

'Did you know they change shells when they get bigger?'

'Yes.'

'Pity it couldn't work for me.'

'Giant clams don't grow in Cornish waters, Hugo, that's the size you'd need.'

'That's as bad as me telling the dachshund he'd be better off with a mineshaft.'

'Sorry, Hugo. What happened next?'

'Well, we get called back in for another session. This time they go on about recognising how there is a power that is greater than us that can restore us to sanity. You can imagine how that went down. Restore a food-addicted dog to sanity? But, I tell you what was interesting. When someone drops an idea in your head it goes to work. Not all at once, but it gets dropped in and, sometimes, like dropping a pebble in a pond, the ripples go out and go to work somewhere.

'At the end of the day I went back to my quarters and had a good think. Now, I'd had a lot of bad luck in me time, but I had also had some good luck. The old soldier had tried to help me, and the only reason he'd failed was me. Then the RNLI had hauled me out of the water, and the staff in the dogs home had been really kind in trying to help me, even though Reggie hadn't succeeded in turning me around. Then I get the luck to go down there. It really was amazing. Best accommodation I had ever had, and even though the grub was a bit lacking in animal protein it wasn't bad. And everybody was trying to help. Thinking about it, it was pretty clear that somebody had faith in me and was trying to sort me out properly. Hugo, my lad, I said to myself, as I drifted off on my bit of memory foam, tomorrow you're going to take this stuff seriously and pay attention.'

'And did you?'

'Of course I didn't. You know what it's like, guv. End of the day, you're tired, you're emotional, and you just want all the bad stuff to stop. Then you have a good night's sleep, because you think you have turned over a new leaf, and when you wake up in the morning, bingo, fresh as a daisy, your first thought is: well, I don't need to start my new life today. I can hack a bit more Jack the Lad before I become Hugo the Labrador Dalai Lama. Thing is, though, the thought has been planted in your head, and when you look back, you can see that that was when it started to germinate and grow. We live in a world, guv, where everyone wants stuff just to happen, at once. But it doesn't. Everything needs time.'

'I agree. We need time to get used to new realities. The Victorians–'

'Guv?'

'Yes?'

'Forgive me for saying this, but you are inclined to get a bit serious. You're much more fun when you're teasing me about giant clam shells than banging on about Victorians.

Now, I don't suppose you've noticed that lunch was a long time ago and home is at least two hours away?'

We walked back to the car. Hugo sat in the back looking out and passing the occasional comment about the countryside. 'Why Suffolk, guv?'

'Named after the south folk.'

'Who were they?'

'They came from a tribe called the Angles, who gave their name to East Anglia and England.'

'Where did they come from, guv?'

'An area called Angeln in Schleswig Holstein, on the borders between Germany and Denmark. They came and settled here after the Romans left.'

'Guv, I'm puzzled.'

'I can see what's coming, Hugo.'

'Are you telling me that the English aren't really English, they're European?'

'Mostly. My ancestors were Danish, probably Viking. The family has been here for at least a thousand years.'

'Guv, at least us dogs just look on ourselves as dogs. Mark you, you might get the odd setter with ideas above his station, and we do have our specialisms, like retrieving if you're a Labrador, or a spot of intimidation if you're a Doberman, but mainly we just muck in and have fun together. The worst problems we have seem to come from our owners – down to us being owner pleasers, I guess. However long I'm a therapist, I'll never get over how strange people are.'

With that we drove home almost in silence. I could see Hugo meditating on the back seat and I could have sworn I heard the chant, 'Om mane padme woof.'

Chapter 7

The Pub Lunch

We both slept in the next day and the sun was well up when we set off up the road to the Heath Extension.

I was keen to hear more of Hugo's story. I was familiar with the twelve-steps process for humans with alcohol addiction, for example, but the idea of calling it "twelve-paws" and applying it to food-addicted dogs was quite novel. Hugo seemed to have mastered the concept of the first two paws, and I was really keen to find out how things progressed.

'Tell me more about your twelve-paws training, Hugo?'

'Everything settled down into a pattern. Lectures on the twelve-paws process. Rather different for dogs than humans, though. They'd get us to sit in rows and recite each paw, and then you'd get a Winalot if you got it right. Didn't take long to get it right that way, but I'm not sure it did much for our addiction. Thing is, you've got to take your time with each one. Take paw three, for example, where you've got to turn your will and life over to your higher power. Us dogs are good on trusting others, but we need a secure pack, doggy or human, around us before we can do that.'

'I think we're the same, Hugo. It's like Maslow's hierarchy of needs: we have to have our basic securities, like food and shelter and safety and love and belonging, before we can start to feel good about ourselves and realise our potential. Now–'

'Guv.'

'Yes, Hugo?'

'I've told you before, you're a nice bloke, but you do have a tendency to get a bit intense and spoil a Labrador's story. And, anyway, whose story is this, and who did psychology at therapist school?'

'Being put back in my box, am I, Hugo?'

'Firmly, guv, firmly. This is my show. I told you right back at the beginning, you listen and then feed me. Now, as I was saying to you before you started wittering on about Maslow, it ain't no use expecting miracles if you are so busy just surviving that you haven't got the mental space to reflect. Something or someone has got to give you that mental space. That's where they were so clever in this retreat. They were really good at making you feel welcome and secure, but they was also very clever with the lectures. I've told you about the ones on the twelve-paws, but there was also ones on life. And for me, they were the ones that finally changed it.

'First up . . . I have got your attention haven't I, guv? Not stealing my thunder doesn't mean it's OK to let your mind wander. This is a therapy session, you know, not just "Hugo Labrador, this is your life".'

'Sorry, Hugo, I thought I saw a Pret wrapper back there.'

At the mention of a Pret wrapper he was gone, tail wagging, nose down across the field we had just walked. He stopped by a group of lads who were flying a drone. It seemed unlikely that they would feed him and he was soon off on his quest again. I walked over to the boys, who had the drone airborne again – and Hugo firmly in their sights as he disappeared behind a hedge. Hugo clearly didn't understand he was being watched because I could see him holding forth with a group of other dogs. They were all very animated, and we carried on watching on the monitor. Eventually the dogs broke up and Hugo came back through the hedge with his customary amiable grin.

'Where have you been, Hugo? Any luck?'

'Luck? Been?'

'You know, the Pret wrapper, and you were out of sight.'

'Oh that, completely forgot, got side-tracked. Met a bunch of me mates and had a quick chinwag. Apparently, they're changing the recycling round around here. Food bins are going to be out on a Thursday.'

'I thought you had your food problems under control?'

'Oh, I have, guv, but some of the youngsters need an eye kept on them, and we had to arrange the fox patrols. Central Square has got a terrible problem with inedible food litter at the moment because of the foxes. Uncooked potatoes and carrots everywhere.

'Now, where was I? Oh yes, the other lectures. They were done by one of the monks. He used to come along and sit with us on the ground and talk to us. Very kind and calm he was, but very strict. No Winalot for being a good boy, it was sit up and pay attention, and you got asked questions about your understanding. He had a good way with words, though. He used to say, "It's no good expecting life to be all good or all bad. It has ups and downs. Sometimes it's good, sometimes it's bad, and that's the way it is. Best way of thinking about it," he said, "is to imagine that it's like a shopping trolley with a wobbly wheel. Not too bad if the ground is smooth, but then, if you put too much in it and go down a narrow aisle, it's quite likely to suddenly take you crashing into the baked beans display." It were a good analogy, I thought. Keep your trolley lightly loaded and accept that it wobbles and then life won't throw any surprises at you. But then he said something else interesting. He said, how much the wobbles bother you depends on how you look at them. If you get upset with every wobble, then your life is going to be a misery; but if you just look at it with a sort of detached amusement, then you see it for what it is: a wobble that will pass.'

'Very profound, Hugo.'

'Not really, guv. I've heard you talking about supermarket queues.'

'Am I allowed to speak?'

'For a bit, but don't bang on.'

'I told you once I used to get very stressed when I had a lot on my plate. I'd always try and find the shortest queue when I had to go to the supermarket, and then get even more stressed when it wouldn't move. One day I thought, I can't do this anymore, so I found the longest queue and read the newspaper whilst I was waiting, and then sometime after that I found I had just slowed right down. I could take any old queue, and I people-watched or chatted. Stress went, and I still got as much done. Truth was, it didn't take much longer just taking a random queue.'

'Exactly, guv, it all depends on how you look at things. So it's not the fault of the cashier, it's not the fault of the lady who has forgotten something and goes back to get it, keeping you waiting, it's just life. Slow down, organise and live in the moment. You could rush through the supermarket, get everything done and paid, get out to your car, and then find there's been an accident and you can't go anywhere anyway. Just look at it a different way, do something useful, and don't think it's a giant conspiracy against you.'

'That's a lot of insight from a Labrador.'

'Took a long time to learn it, guv.'

We walked on up into the trees and across the road. Hugo took off and rootled around in the leaf litter before wandering over to the ponds and looking at the ducks.

'I really like ducks.'

'I'd noticed that. You don't even seem to want to retrieve them?'

'No. I just like watching them. Very peaceful they are. Quite content to dabble away, have the occasional squabble, but basically just spend time chilling out with their mates. Bit of argy-bargy at mating time, but apart from that, nice and peaceful and all contented. Bit like us dogs if we are left alone.'

We carried on over Spaniards Road and onto the Heath proper. Hugo ambled around, tail wagging and generally full of spirits. Suddenly, he came back.

'Guv, can we go somewhere for a sit down? It's me hips. All of a sudden they've let me down, despite me pills. Now, I happen to know there's a little café you like, just over there, so perhaps we could go and 'ave another breakfast. I think I'll feel much better after that, and then perhaps my mistress can come and pick us up.'

'I think you planned this, Hugo.'

'Not at all, guv. You think I would get you to walk all the way to Hampstead for breakfast. Moi? as your French friends would say.'

'Of course I do. You are a cunning, manipulative Labrador, who probably spent half the night laying on his bed thinking about how to get an extra meal. I noticed how little begging or foraging you were doing on the Heath. You had this all worked out.'

The café was just around the corner from the Royal Free Hospital, just up from the Tube station. We had both been there before and they served remarkably good breakfasts.

'What you having, guv, the works? That'll do nicely.'

I rang my friend and she agreed to come and get us, on the promise of a free breakfast. We sat out together on the pavement in the morning sunshine. Hugo looked longingly at the extra plate I had ordered, but even he recognised the "Paddington Bear look" that brooked no interference in his owner's food.

After breakfast we walked the quarter mile back to her car. Hugo grumbled about a lack of door-to-door service – he had become much more vocal about what he did or didn't want to do. He then looked at the jump up from the ground to the floor of the boot, and then back at the two of us.

'Do I have to?' he said. We lifted him in, whereupon he stood up, did a couple of twirls, re-arranged his sleeping bag and settled down happily. 'Just checking you can lift me into the car when I'm in me dotage. Where we going next? How about going down to the river for a late lunch?'

My friend and I looked at each other and burst out laughing.

A couple of hours later we found a vacant table on the terrace of The Dove in Hammersmith, overlooking the river.

Hugo glanced around appreciatively. 'Good view here,' he said, 'lots going on. I like water, always interesting. Do you know, though, sea and rivers is different?'

'We know, Hugo,' we both replied together. 'One is salt, the other's fresh.'

'No, not like that,' said Hugo. 'You're talking to a dog. I can smell and taste the difference. No, they are different metaphors. Go in the sea and the tide will take you out, but, eventually, it will bring you back, not necessarily to the same place, but it will bring you back, whereas a river takes you on a journey. You look over there.'

He pointed to where an eddy had formed just off the main stream. Some rubbish was caught up in it and was slowly rotating. Every so often a piece would escape and rejoin the main flow, only for another piece to be caught and settle to a slow rotation.

'That's a metaphor for what happened to me,' he said. 'I'd been caught up in this river of life, occasionally dumped in a whirlpool and left to go round in circles, and then unceremoniously spat back out into the river again. Current was always too fast to swim against, and I never had the sense to try and drift into the bank and attempt to get out. That takes some doing, too. You ever tried it, guv?'

'Only once, when I was tipped into a river when the bank gave way beneath me. Nearly died, until I found a tree root I could get my arm round. Had a hell of a struggle getting out.'

'You know what it's like, then. Well, the way I looked at it, my stay in Cornwall was like being washed up at a landing stage – you know, one of those that slopes into the water, slippery at first, and partly in the water, and then the further out you get the easier it becomes. I thought I'd done all the bit about sitting around talking about me problems, and what I needed was to find a new way of living me life. That's where the lectures came in so handy. I've said before that the thing about alcohol and drugs is that you have got to give 'em up to make any progress. You'll always have the addiction, that doesn't go away, but at least if you stop taking them a lot of the bad stuff eases after a while.

'With food you can't give it up, you have to look at it in a different way. What it took me a very long time to learn was the importance of the right owner. Us dogs is pack animals, and we do pack much better than self. Now, when you are an addict, it's all about self. Very dangerous concept self. All sorts of problems flow from thinking self. But if you think "we" or "my pack", and get the right owner, they will give you tough love and keep you away from food. Sort of a case of, you can keep the food away from a Labrador, but you can't keep a Labrador away from his food drive. Trouble was, I had such a horrible reputation, so how was I to get the right owner?'

'You must have had a terrible time.'

'It weren't good. But I'm getting hungry with all this talking. Can we have a look at the "me and you?"'

We showed Hugo the menu.

The Chiswick lifeboat drifted slowly down the river, taking care not to produce any wash and upset the rowers who were out on the water.

Hugo glanced up, was about to say something, but returned to his menu. 'Wish they would make them dog-friendly, guv.'

'In what way?'

'Well, it would be ever so handy if someone just stuck a thumb in the food and then squished their thumb by the description. As a dog I would get far more information that way than by reading the description.'

'Brilliant idea, Hugo, but it would make the menus look a bit dog-eared – no pun intended.'

'That's not a pun, guv, that's where the phrase came from. It would be helpful, though. I could tell you how long the steak had been aged, what the chips had been fried in – I hate corn oil by the way –and how long the cod had been battered by a frontier. What is frontier-battered, by the way?'

'It's a beer batter, where the beer used is called Frontier. It's a craft ale, I think. Could be wrong, though.'

'Well, I could tell you how long the batter had been made before they used it. It changes smell quite quickly, you know.'

'Really?'

'Honest, guv. Do they do a tasting menu? If I could have a little bit of everything as a starter, then I could advise you on your choice and make up me mind what I really wanted.'

I could hear Hugo's mistress silently sobbing with laughter. 'Is this how you two boys spend your days out?' she eventually asked. 'I'm beginning to understand why Hugo has been putting on weight since you came to stay!'

Hugo and I looked at each other sheepishly.

'Certainly not,' I said, feeling, as I said so, the colour of my cheeks rising.

'You always blushed, even as a boy,' she said. 'I can see you two have a great time.'

Hugo just looked on. The only betrayal of his impassivity was the lengthening string of drool as he mentally contemplated his lunch.

We ordered our food, and Hugo was given his midday portion of Obesity Management for dogs in his travelling dog bowl.

'Guv?'

'Hugo?'

'Me patience is ever so tested.'

'By what, Hugo?'

'The lack of variety in me lunch. I had hopes, you know.'

'You did have breakfast.'

'I also had dreams.'

'But you were the one who brought up the subject of tough love. You told me you had found your right owner, eventually.'

'Humph.'

His lunch finished he got up, walked to the full extent of his lead and flopped back down so he could survey the river from the top of the terrace steps. I moved my chair to trap the end of his lead under my chair leg. I wasn't taking any chances.

Hugo sighed again. 'Don't know why I bother being a therapist Labrador if I'm not trusted.'

And with that he went into a sulk that persisted all the way home.

Later that day, Hugo and I took his mistress to the airport for her regular trip to Prague. On returning home, we went for a walk, but Hugo stayed silent. It was only later, when I had settled down in an armchair and put my feet up in front of the fire, that he came over.

'You were a bit tough on me, guv, you know.'

'You're a rascal. I know you have made huge progress with your insight, but you also know that it's being in a tough, loving pack that keeps you on the straight and narrow.'

'Interesting isn't it, guv. Shades of John Donne, really: "No man is an island" – or, in this case, dog. I know that if I was back on me own, fending for myself, I would be back with me addiction. We all need our pack around us. You do, I do. We can't survive on our own, it all goes wrong. But the pack needs to be OK. It's not good enough for it just to be a pack. It's got to be a good pack. You get a bunch of bad dogs together and everything gets very scary. The bad reinforces the bad. Works the other way with the good. You get a good bunch of dogs, or dogs and humans together, and you get fantastic bonds.'

'You know, there is a phrase that "neurons that wire together, fire together". In other words, if you keep on consciously, or even unconsciously, thinking the same things your brain changes so that those thoughts become hard-wired for you. It's a really important concept.'

A gentle snore came from the hearth rug. I didn't need reminding. I had become a bit 'serious' again and strayed into his territory. He wasn't one for discussion. When he listened, and observed, he did it very intently, but it always had to be Hugo that made the running. I quietly turned off the fire and turned out the light. I tiptoed to the door.

I was just leaving the room when, 'Forgotten something, have we?'

'Don't think so.'

'Night-time snack.'

'Night-time snack?'

'You know, guv, that regular little tribute to me innards that induces the state of relaxation and sweet dreams that my mistress normally provides me with.'

'Don't know anything about it, Hugo, but you can have a couple of Winalot.'

'Guv, you're a star. I like the ones that are fish-shaped, if you don't mind. Can you save the charcoal ones for when I have a bad gut?'

And with that we went to bed. I dreamt of a Labrador sitting in the candlelight reading John Donne. I was beginning to seriously doubt my sanity.

Chapter 8

A Rainy Day

The next day it rained. Apart from walks around Bigwood in the morning and afternoon, Hugo and I stayed in all day. I decided to do some batch cooking for the freezer. Hugo alternated between his bed and under my feet whilst I cooked.

'Not sure about that raw onion, guv. It was a bit fierce. Are you going to cook it?'

'Of course. You didn't have to eat it.'

'It's a habit.'

'Try breaking it.'

'Difficult.'

'I'd noticed.'

'You need to fry off that mince a bit longer. Not enough caramel in the smell.'

'Thank you.'

'Shouldn't have put quite so much mixed Italian herbs in. Can't take 'em out now.'

'Thank you for the glimpse of the obvious.'

'Just trying to be helpful.'

'Why don't you distract yourself?'

'How, with all the cooking smells going on? You put the right amount of passata and beef stock in, by the way.'

'Tell me some more about your time in Soho.'

'It weren't all bad. For a while Bonzo, Marmalade, Zoe and I had a lovely time. I used to sleep down in the theatre, as I told you. Marmalade lived in the lamp shop in Berwick Street, and Bonzo went home at night. His owners were out all day and trusted him with a dog flap to his rather palatial kennel. The flap must have been the size of a door, but he had a chip on his collar to let him in and out. A lot of the time we would all hang out for the evening in the lamp shop. Zoe would sometimes join us on her way back from the drawing classes.

'There were a lot of interesting characters around then. One of them was called Old Christmas, no Mr or Father, just plain Old Christmas. He sometimes came and sat by the fire with us in the back of the shop. He was old when we knew him, and he was one of those people who was always around but you never knew anything about him. We didn't know where he lived, or if he was on his own, he was just around. For most of the year he worked as a sort of market porter – he helped the traders with their stalls in Berwick Street. Lunchtime would find him sitting on his own in one of the local Soho pubs, quietly drinking a pint and watching the world from his bar stool. He always had a smile on his face, and lovely warm eyes that made you think you were the only creature in the world. We always used to worry that he was lonely, and I think in some ways he was, but he never let on and always seemed so happy with everybody he met.' Hugo sniffed. 'More seasoning with that and it should be just about right. Don't put the basil in too early, mind.'

'Hugo, one day I'll throw this at you.'

'Can't wait, guv. Why do you think I pester you? Oi, you didn't need to kick me toy zebra at me. I'm offended.'

'Hugo, will you please get out from under my feet. Go back to your bed and get on with your story.'

'Can I have a Winalot?'

'One.'

'Only one?'

'Unless the story is very good.'

'Humph. Suppose you're going to put this in your book?'

'I might. Go on. I'm really interested.'

'You like local colour, don't you?'

'Yes. I also find Soho fascinating. There is so much history there, and I love the fact that so many of the old buildings survive, some of them, like the lamp shop, almost unaltered. Tell me more about Old Christmas.'

'Well, Old Christmas used to tell us the most amazing stories about Father Christmas. Claimed he was his brother, but none of us believed him. He used to tell us of the problems Father Christmas was having now up in the Arctic. How he'd had to put the whales to work pushing the ice floes together to make a long enough runway for his sled, and how he had the polar bears harnessed to rollers to flatten the ice for him.

'The story I liked best was about Father Christmas's filing system. Seems there is an Arctic creature bit like a small whale, with a single tusk, called a narwhal, apparently. According to Old Christmas, he'd have a whole pod of narwhals lined up along the ice and he'd spike notes to himself on their tusks about all the Christmas presents he had to deliver. They were good stories and we always loved hearing them.

'At Christmas time, Old Christmas would pull out a Santa outfit and a white beard and go and work in one of the posh department stores. It was the only time of the year when he really came alive. He absolutely loved it, and he'd come back and tell us about all the little kids he had met during the day and how much fun it was.'

'Someone had a fertile imagination there, Hugo. Sure you hadn't overdosed on cheese?'

'Certainly not. One Christmas we missed him. He was here one day and not here the next. Then came the sad news that he'd been found really ill down at the bottom of Berwick Street. They'd taken him down to St Thomas's but to no avail. Rumour has it he said to the staff, "Don't worry, my dears, I shall be quite alright," and he smiled at them with those amazing eyes and died.

'It turned out he had been an actor when he was very young and it hadn't really worked out. He rented a single room off someone in Wardour Street and just quietly went about his business. No family – that is if you don't count the street family that he had in our bit of Soho. We had a memorial service for him in St Paul's, Covent Garden – you know, the actor's church – late one evening before Christmas. We all went and gave him a good send off, with many a tear and fond reminiscence. Bonzo, Marmalade and I were the last to leave.

'Just as we came out Marmalade suddenly says, "Look, up there!" We looked up and, blow me, there was a sled with its reindeers in the sky. And you know what? There was Father Christmas holding the reins, and right beside him was Old Christmas. He just looked at us and smiled and said, "Told you I'd be alright. Stay safe, my dears," and then they vanished. I always believed in Father Christmas after that.'

'You're an old softie.'

'I tell you what, guv, when you were living the sort of life I was then, having a place of sanctuary for a bit and someone to tell you nice stories was very special. Don't knock it.'

'Sorry, Hugo.'

'There were others around as well, bit like Old Christmas. Most of them were lonely, but nice people. We always tried to look after each other. We all had our problems and our history. The old soldier was one of them. He'd seen a lot of stuff he shouldn't. Couldn't get it out of his head and couldn't talk about it. Used to have terrible dreams. Some nights he would just get up and pace around the bedroom in his flat. He used to swear something awful, and his rages . . . well. He never harmed anybody, though. His cat and I used to try and help him, but he was in a world of his own. He wouldn't lay down until he exhausted himself, and then his cat would curl up on his belly and I'd sit by his side and let him rest his hand on me head. He liked that. I still feel terrible about letting 'im down.'

'You were ill too, Hugo. You still are. Don't beat yourself up.'

'I know, guv, but I did try to help. It's shocking how little people get helped who really need it. There's an old bit of verse from hundreds of years back, about how we forget soldiers.

'Don't know that.'

'You should, guv. Look it up. Nothing changes. The old soldier used to quote it under his breath most days, and particularly when he went down to the Guards Memorial:

"When war's proclaimed and danger's nigh
God and the soldier is the peoples 'cry
When war is ov'r, and all things righted
God's forgotten, and the soldier slighted."

***

'Sometimes he'd just stand there, and his shoulders would droop, and the tears would run down his face as he looked at that memorial. I didn't know what to do, except lean up against him. Then he'd pull himself together, look at me and say, "No slacking now, young Hugo." And he'd square his shoulders back, stick his chest out and march us home. Didn't have no friends apart from his cat and me, and I was no use in the end. Shocking the lack of care for him. He was another one like Old Christmas. He'd sit in a pub at lunch time with a pint in front of him, all on his own. The Sun and Thirteen Cantons were his favourite. You know, the pub in Great Pulteney Street. Named after all the Swiss that used to live round there. Soho got called the Thirteenth Canton.'

'I didn't know any of that, Hugo.'

'Well, you should. Much more important than you spoiling a good bit o' mince by cooking it. You could just put it in me bowl raw, you know.'

'Not all of us share your taste in food, Hugo. Anyway, raw mince is not that appetising with pasta.'

Hugo groaned. 'Me nemesis – if you don't count chocolate cake, that is. I've only got to look at pasta and the weight goes on. Shocking it is, shocking.'

'Well, I tell you what, you let me cook and I'll let you reminisce.'

'Deal, but how about another Winalot?'

'OK. Last one, though.'

'Spoilsport.'

Hugo fell silent and gazed gloomily out of the window at the rain, which was now coming down steadily.

'Looks set in for the day,' he remarked. 'Think I'll go out this afternoon, anyway.'

'What's with the, "I'll go out"? You know your mistress would kill me if I let you out on the streets on your own.'

'Yes,' said Hugo, 'bit ironic that, given me past don't you think.'

'That's as maybe, but I'm not chancing you scarpering off and resuming picnic-robbing on Hampstead Heath. We'll go together.'

'I'm happy to go me own, you'll only get wet, guv.'

'Hugo, it's worth a bit of wet to keep you on the straight and narrow.'

'Given up picnic-robbing, anyway. That was a long time ago.'

'Glad to hear it.'

He settled back on his bed and pretended to go to sleep, but one half-opened eye followed me around the kitchen.

'What you doing now?'

'Clearing up.'

He was by my side in a flash.

'Can I lick the saucepan?'

'That's unhygienic.'

'Not if you put it through the dishwasher.'

'No space, it's too big.'

''Er Ladyship lets me.'

'No, she doesn't, and she particularly told me about this ploy.'

'Humph, shan't tell you any more stories.'

'That's OK. Shan't give you any more Winalot.'

A sigh came from his bed, followed by pretend snores.

I finished tidying up the kitchen and put on a coat and fetched Hugo's lead. The beady eye followed me, but his body didn't move an inch.

'I'm not going out in this.'

'You are.'

'I shall catch me death.'

'You were all set to go on your own.'

'That's different.'

'Why?'

'No good reason. Just not going out.'

'No supper, then.'

Hugo grudgingly got off his bed and flopped by the front door. I clipped his lead on. With studied weariness he stood in the porch, watching the rain.

'I hate rain.'

'How did you cope when you were on the streets?'

'Stood in a doorway like this.'

'What happened when you got hungry?'

'Had to go out then. Were some benefits, though. The kitchen staff were always in a hurry to get back in themselves, so they tended just to chuck the waste food in the general direction of the bin. You could get a good feed that way.'

'Want me to try rain with your supper?'

'No. It would get a bit soggy. That were always the problem round the back of a Chinese. Soggy rice noodles were disgusting, even for an addict. There was always guaranteed pickings because of the volume of waste, but if it got wet and soggy . . .'

'Hugo, you're putting me off food.'

'Good, just pass down what you've been cooking, then, and we'll pass on the walk.'

I closed the front door behind us and turned up my collar. Hugo stood in the front porch in dismay now his retreat had been cut off.

'You're serious about this, aren't you?'

'Yep.'

With much grumbling we set off. We had the wood to ourselves. The trees gave some protection, but Hugo now decided that he really did want a walk and everything had to be explored and sniffed. He moved at a snail's pace, with the consequence that we got wetter and wetter. The walk turned into a battle of wills: he was willing me to break for home, which would mean a quick rub down, which he always liked, and then a meal.

'Aren't you wet?'

'Getting that way, but skin is waterproof. What's your coat like?'

'A bit damp. Getting heavier.'

'Does that mean you want to go home?'

'I'll survive.'

The battle was on, and we carried on trudging round the perimeter of the wood.

'I suppose we've passed the point of no return?'

'As in it's quicker to go on than go back?'

'Yes.'

'I think so, what would you like to do?'

Rather than admit defeat Hugo closed right in and deliberately walked just in front of me, at a pace that was just too slow. Eventually we got home.

'Don't suppose you've got any hot food, guv?'

'You've had a rub down, you've got a radiator, you've had food and you're a dog.'

'I shall ignore that last disparaging remark. Always used to get hot food when I was running me sledging rescue team in Labrador.'

''You've spent too much time daydreaming on your bed today. It's a good story, though.'

'They really did have sledge rescue teams, you know. They trialled dropping 'em out of aeroplanes and off they went into the Canadian wilderness. 1952 it were. Didn't use parachutes, neither.'

'Very impressive, Hugo.'

'You know why they didn't use Labradors?'

'No.'

'We needed too many rations. Turned out huskies were better suited. Shame that, it would have been a real badge of honour amongst us Labradors. Awesome dogs, huskies.'

'I know, Hugo.'

'If I'd been born a husky I wouldn't have been a food addict. I sometimes think it were bad luck I were born a Labrador.'

'You make up for it in other ways.'

'I know, by helping people and doing toilet roll ads. It would be nice to be known for doing stuff that's heroic.'

''Can't all be action dogs. Anyway, you're supposed to be a dog therapist, and you can talk. Those are seriously impressive achievements.'

'Not when you really want to be a sledge rescue leader.'

'"They also serve who stand and wait . . ."'

'Been brushing up on your Milton, guv?'

'Something like that.'

'Can I have me tea?'

'You just did.'

'Spoilsport.'

And with that Hugo twirled around in his bed and went to sleep.

I tiptoed out of the kitchen, not forgetting to shut all the cupboard doors and push any food on the counter right to the back.'

'You could have left me just a little opportunity, guv.'

'Not a chance, Hugo, not a chance.'

***

Later that evening Hugo ambled through into the sitting room.

'What yer up to?'

'Reading.'

'Reading what?'

'Pellegrino Artusi's Science in the Kitchen and the Art of Eating Well.'

'Best Italian cookbook ever. Know what I like?'

'No.'

'The way he discusses the dishes as well as giving you the recipe. Makes for interesting reading on the rare occasions when I have a full stomach and time to reflect.'

'Perhaps not the best way for a food addict to pass the time. Rather like giving an alcoholic a wine list, I would have thought. Feeling hungry?'

'I did just come in to be sociable, but now you mention it.'

'Remind me, when did you last eat?'

'Breakfast.'

'Which one?'

Hugo looked crestfallen. 'Third breakfast.'

'So that would be about two hours ago?'

'Suppose so.'

'So it's just a night-time snack, then.'

'It's a proper meal.'

'Pull the other one.'

''Er Ladyship gives me a meal.'

'No, she doesn't.'

'Nobody loves Labradors, and after all the love and affection we give you . . .'

'That's emotional blackmail, and you know it isn't true.'

'Worth a try.'

'Good night, Hugo.'

Chapter 9

The Lake District

We had the next few days on our own. My friend was in Prague so Hugo and I went to my brother's caravan in the Lake District for a few nights. This was Hugo's first adventure north of Watford Gap and he was very excited. He sat on the seat behind me looking out at the passing countryside. We had the usual conversation about place names, explanations of Northampton and Warwickshire, and entreaties to stop at every motorway service station that had a McDonalds. Hugo had a new scam going: he had started collecting themed food wrappers and he was currently working his way through McDonalds' breakfasts. He maintained his little collection on the wall in the corner by his bed in the kitchen and, when out of sorts with the world, would lie flat out, with his nose against them, and a forlorn look on his face. Today was going to be the double bacon and egg McMuffin meal as far as Hugo was concerned. I didn't mind him adding the wrapper to his collection, but as he had recently been diagnosed with gallstones a wary eye on his food intake was the order of the day. We stopped briefly at Northampton to "ease springs" and add to Hugo's collection.

'Guv?'

'Yes?'

'You going to go "large" on that?'

'No, only on the coffee.'

'Can I have your hash brown?'

'No, but you can have my egg.'

We went back to the car. I got Hugo's food out of his travelling case, poured in the regulation portion of Obesity Management, added water, and put his egg on top.

'Quite the gourmet presentation,' Hugo remarked, sarcastically. 'Your take on an Île flottante with the amount of water you've put in.'

I ignored him. I folded the new wrapper and put it in his travelling case.

'Another one for the collection, Hugo.'

'Humph.'

Hugo jumped back into the car and settled down. We set off.

'Wake me up when we get to Spaghetti Junction.'

'I was trying to keep quiet about that in case it gave you a problem.'

'Did me research, didn't I. You thought I was going to have a crisis, go all snowflake on you. Well, you might like to know I don't get on with spaghetti; frightful stuff the way it hangs out of your mouth and falls to the ground when you take a bite. If I had opposable thumbs I could manage a fork, but seeing as how I haven't, I stick to macaroni or lasagne.'

A groan then came from the back of the car.

'How long till lunch, guv?'

'You've just had breakfast.'

'No. What I had was what you, with your posh French way of describing things, call a "bonne bouche". Breakfast is two eggs, two rashers of bacon, two sausages, two field mushrooms, two tins of baked beans, two portions of hash browns, two tomatoes, two Loch Fyne kippers–'

'Enough, Hugo, lunch is over three hours away. We have some distance to cover.'

Some muttering came from the back of the car and then Hugo settled again.

As we were passing the turning for Middlewich he stirred once more.

'See the sign? That turn off reminds me of a story. Met an old lurcher once. Named Nimrod. He'd come into the Berwick Street lamp shop with his master, who wanted to have a poke around. Funny bloke, seemed a bit disappointed there weren't any acetylene lamps. Tried telling him they were all either for candles or electrics, but he wouldn't listen.

'Anyway, this old lurcher and I were discussing grub. "Hugo," he said, "you need to watch out as you get older. Sense of smell starts to go and you get a bit confused. I got taken to a race meeting at Oulton Park once. Got the smell of fried bread and Bovril confused with castor oil. Nearly got run over. Had a paw in plaster and me head in a radar dish for weeks after that." Anyway, thought you might like that story to help you stay awake. The car is beginning to sway a bit – you can tell when you're in the back.'

Hugo drifted off again. We were making good time, and with Hugo sleeping I pushed on. We stopped for a late lunch at Lancaster and, after the usual grumbles about variety and portion size, continued towards our destination.

'Can I have some?'

'Have some what?'

'Mint cake.'

Unbeknownst to me, Hugo had surfaced and was looking at the road signs again.

''Hugo, were you born with a food map of England in your head?'

'Everybody has heard of Kendal Mint Cake. Used to be in sledging rations in Labrador. It's a great cure for dog breath, you know.'

'And a great disaster for dog teeth, I'm sure. Not long to go now.'

Soon the road started to climb and I saw in the distance the looming bulk of Shap and the turn off for Tebay.

'One last stop for provisions before we get to the caravan.'

Hugo sat up. 'Can I choose?'

'You aren't allowed in the food hall, but we will treat ourselves to a couple of proper breakfasts and some steaks for our supper. It won't all be Obesity Management, I promise you.'

Hugo acquiesced. 'I'll stay here and watch the ducks then,' he said, and settled back in the car.

When I returned, he said, 'Guv?'

'Yes?'

'Am I getting sticky toffee pudding?'

'You're not, no.'

'Is that oak-smoked back bacon?'

'Yes.'

'Can I have some?'

'Tomorrow.'

'Champion. Is that a dry-aged T-bone steak I'm smelling?'

'How do you get so much detail, Hugo?'

'It's a bit like the Sami, guv, the herders in northern Scandinavia, they have about 300 words for types of snow and ice. Us dogs are similar for meat smells, only more so.'

After the service station the road climbed up and over Shap. We left the motorway at Penrith and followed the signs for Ullswater. Arriving at the caravan I parked up and took Hugo for a walk before unlocking. It had been a long time in the car for him and we were both tired, but equally keen to stretch our legs before settling in for the rest of the day.

We sat on a bench looking at the lake below us.

'Fancy a decent walk tomorrow?'

'Would that be one of those walks where you do a packed lunch for both of us and we stop at a café if we find one?'

'That would be the one. But this time we also get to go on one of the lake ferries.'

'What's a ferry?'

'It's a passenger boat that picks you up and drops you off at various points on the lake. You can then walk from where you have been dropped off to another ferry point, or even home. I thought we might take the ferry from Glenridding across to Howtown, and then walk back to Glenridding again. It will be a good day.'

'You're on. Now can we have supper?'

I unlocked the caravan. My brother and his wife had owned it for years and it was very much a family favourite. I carried our bags in whilst Hugo smelt around.

'Your brother have a poodle?'

'Yes, I think I told you a few weeks ago.'

An anguished howl came from the sitting room. I went in quickly to see what the matter was. Hugo was sitting disconsolately in front of a photograph of my brother's old poodle, who had died a few years before.

'Guv, that looks just like Zoe!' Hugo sobbed.

I felt absolutely terrible. It hadn't occurred to me that there would be photos of my brother's dog around, and Hugo's memories of his lost love had been very firmly reawakened. I didn't tell Hugo that the dog in the photo was also called Zoe. Not just then. I sat down beside him and gave him a cuddle.

'Want to talk about it?'

Hugo nodded. 'Tell me about the dog in the picture, guv.'

'She was my brother's dog. She died some years ago. My brother got her as a rescue dog. She'd had several litters and was then abandoned and then rescued. My brother and his wife are great dog lovers; the vet said their rescue poodle couldn't have found a better home.'

'What was she called?'

'A bit tricky this, Hugo . . . Zoe.'

'Guv, she looks so much like my Zoe, love of my life she were. Where does your brother live?'

'Just outside Liverpool.'

Another sob came from Hugo. 'My Zoe came from Liverpool. I wonder if they're related?'

'I don't know, Hugo, there can't be too many beautiful white standard poodles in Liverpool.'

'Guv, I got to find her. Can we ask your brother to help?'

I could not ignore the pleading eyes. Every Labrador does pleading eyes, but Hugo could do them in spades. I couldn't let him down. I agreed.

'We'll start tomorrow, Hugo. We'll have to go out from here to get a mobile signal, though, and I'll start by calling my brother.'

Fortunately, I was able to keep an eye on Hugo whilst I cooked supper. He lay sprawled across the floor gazing at the picture, in a complete reverie. He didn't stir when I started grilling the steak, although I could see his nose starting to twitch. He didn't respond to the clatter of saucepans, or the sound of me putting a plate on the table. He watched me put his food down, and then cut some steak onto another plate for him to have after his normal meal. He watched me eat. This was a side to Hugo I had never seen before. He had talked about Zoe when we walked through Kensington, but that had been with an air of fond reminiscence. This was different. He was completely knocked sideways by seeing the picture. Here was something that, at least for the moment, was bigger than food.

Eventually, he raised himself from his reverie and came and ate.

'Guv?'

'Yes, Hugo?'

'You mean it about trying to find Zoe?'

'Of course. It won't be easy, though. Finding dogs can be even harder than finding people. But I know my brother will do his best.'

'Can I have a Facebook page? She might be on Facebook.'

'When we get back to London.'

We sat on the decking at the back of the caravan until it was dark and the midges drove us in. Later still, sitting at the little dining table, we watched a badger trying to get peanuts from the bird feeder. Hugo was very excited.

'That what I think it is?'

'A badger.'

'Yes, never seen one before.'

I got into bed. Hugo crashed out in his sofa-bed that he had insisted we bring with us. It filled half the car, but he was very proud of it. "Best Orvis Labrador tartan," he'd said, "and memory foam".

'What does the memory foam remember, Guv?'

'You, Hugo.'

'Wish it could remember Zoe.'

'So do I, Hugo. Night-night.'

There was a sob, closely followed by snoring. I went to sleep.

***

Hugo woke me around six thirty.

'Come on, guv,' he said, 'time for breakfast, lots to do today. Big walk and poodle-finding.'

I let him out and went and made coffee.

'Where's the full English, then?'

'Give me a break, Hugo, it takes time.' I opened the door from the kitchenette onto the decking. Hugo lay across the threshold in the morning sun. Birds hopped on and off the feeders by the bushes. The smell of bacon and eggs wafted its way past Hugo's nose.

'We are on holiday aren't we, guv?'

'Yes.'

'So, there will be the odd meal that isn't entirely Obesity Management for dogs?'

'There will.'

'Promise?'

'I promise, and it starts in just a moment.'

Quick as a flash Hugo was round, the morning's tranquillity broken.

'What am I having for breakfast?'

'Obesity Management for dogs!' we chorused, and then I added, 'Plus an egg, a slice of black pudding and half a sausage.'

'Guv, you're a star, couldn't make it a whole sausage, could you?'

'No, Hugo, I daren't. You're going to have to walk an extra five miles today to get rid of this as it is.'

By eight thirty breakfast was over and the pans and plates washed and put away and the caravan tidied. Hugo was keen to get moving, so we packed our things for the day and drove down to Glenridding. We had a while to wait for the first ferry. Hugo wanted to get on with finding Zoe, so I rang my brother and discussed the problem with him. He replied with his customary, "Leave it with me, bro, I'll have a think and get back to you."

I returned to Hugo.

'I've done all I can for the moment. My brother is looking up how to find a standard white poodle.'

'That's absolutely beautiful, guv.'

'I'll make certain he looks for an absolutely beautiful standard white poodle.'

The ferry arrived at the pier and we made our way to the foredeck. Hugo sat in the bow, looking across the lake. The ferry departed with a blast on the horn, and soon picked up speed. Hugo's nose went slightly higher into the air and his nostrils started twitching. His ears lifted in the breeze.

'I like this, guv.'

'I can see.'

'Is that a hotel over there?'

'It is.'

'Supper should be good there tonight.'

'How so?'

'They're making a slow beef reduction, I can smell it – bones, marrow, bits of shin, few chef's veggies.'

'You can get all that from a couple of miles away?'

'Easy, guv. I could get that in London when there were hundreds of hotels around. Could tell which the best ones were too.'

'You never cease to amaze me.'

The sun sparkled over the water behind us. We shared an ice cream – or rather Hugo ate the bits I dropped. The ferry stopped at Aira Force, and then chugged on to Howtown, where we got off.

'We've got quite a way to go, Hugo. I've got a packed lunch for both of us.'

'Guv?'

'Yes?'

'That hotel over there, can we see what's for elevenses? It is a holiday.'

We made for the walker's bar. I found Hugo some water and we shared a plate of cheese and pickle sandwiches. Finally, we got on our way.

'When am I going to hear about Zoe, guv?'

'Don't know, Hugo. My brother will look into it and he'll let us know. I expect I shall hear something before the end of the day.'

We walked on in silence, skirting round the back of Hallin Fell and walking on down to Sandwick.

'Hugo, I'm intrigued. Tell me more about your time in Cornwall?'

''Inquisitive, are we?'

'I guess so, but it is a very unusual story.'

'Hmm. You like philosophy, guv?'

'I think you know the answer to that.'

'It took me a while to realise, but we had a very strict structure to our day. The timings varied a bit, though, according to the state of the tide, because we always had our exercise on the beach. Got to know the beach very well. I had favourite spots where I could go and look in the rock pools. Loved them, I did. It's funny, you know, you sit and watch this separate world going on. You can't live in there and they can't live out here. The little hermit crabs, the anemones, the little fish – they just carry on as if we weren't there. Sometimes you overstep the mark and let your shadow fall over them and then everything stops, they vanish. Then, if you sit patiently again, they all come out and get on with their lives. It's a sort of metaphor really: be patient, observe, live and let live, and everything seems quite happy. Got so absorbed one day nearly got cut off by the tide. Had to swim for it and was nearly late for me class. They still made me go to the class, too. Very strict they were, and very uncomfortable and wet was I. Didn't do it again. I learnt me lesson. Always puzzled by the tides, though. They seemed to change in time each day.'

'I'll tell you about tides one day. Tell me more about the lessons?'

'Told you before, combination of the twelve-paws and lectures on philosophy. Next up was making a searching and fearless moral inventory of meself. That weren't hard for me. I'd never been in denial about me problems. Lot of the other dogs were, though. They couldn't see that they had done bad stuff and were addicted to food. It was like they had built this protective wall up around themselves; sort of exoskeleton to hold everything in. Break that and they'd all come flopping out and need rebuilding. Trouble was, how were they going to do that? You've opened a packet by mistake and then tried to put everything back as it was and found it didn't work? It's a scary thought if you are that packet, and life isn't so bad for you at the moment. Break the packet open, and there's no knowing where the contents will spill, or what it will be like when you try and put it back together. Much better just to jolly along as you are. It's back to having to really, really want to get better yourself. Nobody can do that for you.

'Anyway, I made me fearless searching moral inventory. Basically: kind-hearted Labrador who is completely unable to turn down a food opportunity. Will beg, borrow or steal to get food. Happy-go-lucky, except when the hunger pangs start, generally about ten minutes after the last meal. Diagnosis: food addict. Statement of needs: strong, loving, disciplined pack that remove opportunities out of me way, feed me regularly, occasionally give the odd treat, and generally keep me on the straight and narrow. Availability of such pack: box ticked for present whilst in sanctuary. Long term future: decidedly dodgy unless I can find a further pack when I leave, but perhaps they could give me some help. You can see how difficult it all was.'

'I can, Hugo.'

'Well, next up it were back to the fifth and sixth paw, and turning myself over to a higher power, and another about the exact nature of me wrongs and being ready for me higher power to remove me shortcomings. That was tricky. I had no problem turning myself over and being ready to remove me shortcomings. I was even ready for it, which was the seventh paw. I'd have loved to be free from me food addiction, be like one of those dogs where you could put a plate of food down and leave it alone until the owner says, "'Good boy." Always thought that was a bit like a circus act. I had the insight, and I wanted the cure . . . I just felt I knew myself too well and, given half an opportunity, I'd be straight back to square one.'

'But isn't that back to the importance of having the right pack around you for support, Hugo?'

'Course it is, guv. But it's also about learning to be able to trust yourself. It all takes time. You said it yourself: neurons that fire together wire together. It takes time to develop new patterns and bed them in. Fortunately, that was what the sanctuary was giving me. Now, I've talked long enough. I happen to know that there is a spare cheese and pickle sandwich in your backpack.'

We had reached Roscombe Rigg. I had a dilemma. Given a chance, Hugo would consume all his rations at the beginning of the walk and would then stage a sit-down strike, saying he couldn't go on, it was unfair on a Labrador, how was he expected to cope, he was a town dog, not one of these marathon-running border collies he'd seen chasing over the hills . . .

'How come they've got a licence to chase sheep, guv?' he'd remarked earlier.

'Because they've been trained.'

'Who'd want to chase sheep, anyway?' said Hugo. 'Much easier to empty bins.'

My look told him he'd overstepped the mark.

'Sorry, guv, only joking.'

'Hugo, a couple of Winalot and we'll stop when we get to Birkfell Slack, how about that?'

'Mustn't grumble,' came the reply. 'Guv?'

'Yes, Hugo?'

'I like watching border collies.'

'Yes, Hugo.'

'Did you ever watch "One Man and his Dog"?'

'Never missed it.'

'Jolly clever, I thought, all that racing around the hills with a "Come bye" and "Away!"'

'Yes, Hugo.'

'Can I have a go whilst we're up here?'

'What, Hugo the famous Labrador explorer, trying his hand at a bit of organised sheep exercising?'

'Doesn't really work does it, guv?'

'No, not really.'

'Can I try it with running ducks, like they do at country shows?'

'Didn't know you'd seen that?'

'Only on the telly. Love to give it a go in real life. I like ducks.'

We entered the trees and started to climb up, away from the lake. The first of the more spirited walkers started to appear, going the other way. As ever Hugo was straight over, with a wag and a smile, trying to beg the odd morsel. As ever, nine times out of ten he succeeded.

'Friendly dog! I like Labradors!' would come the greeting.

Who doesn't? I'd think. 'Oh, very friendly, one of the best. He's a bit of a scrounger, I'm afraid,' I'd say.

'Oh, don't mind him. Can I give him a bit of my sandwich?'

'Of course, but no Kendal Mint Cake. Good for breath, bad for teeth.'

And we would have a quick laugh over that, and then they would be gone.

'I'll have you know, guv, that I'm not that fond of Kendal Mint Cake.'

'Really?'

'Really. You know how you use menthol crystals when your nose is blocked up?'

'Yes.'

'And you know how it cuts through everything, and everything smells of menthol?'

'Yes.'

'Same thing with Kendal Mint Cake. But imagine it when you've got a nose that's a thousand times more sensitive. As me Auntie Elly says, "It plays havoc with me olfactories."'

'I'd never thought about it like that.'

'You should be a bit more thoughtful. How am I supposed to know whether or not someone has got their lunch with them if all I can smell is peppermint?'

And with that, we carried on. At last the path turned downhill again, and we crossed Birkfell Slack and went to find somewhere to sit in the sun, near the water's edge. We looked across the water. The steamer plied its business taking folk around the lake. Hugo was fascinated.

'Never seen a lake this big. How big is it?'

'About the same as the distance from the centre of Golders Green to Bermondsey.'

'Have they got a lifeboat?'

''Fraid not, Hugo, you'll have to wait for our next seaside trip.'

'I like lifeboats, guv. Wish I could be like Station Dog George at Aldeburgh. He's a real hero of mine.'

'Didn't know you'd met him.'

'Oh, I haven't, but he's very famous. He's part of the reason I want to be on Facebook, so I can be a friend of his.'

We finished our lunch with the usual chorus of, 'Do you have to eat your crusts?' and 'I've had enough Obesity Management for dogs, can't you do a pomodoro rusticana and basil sauce?' and then, finally, 'How about just one Winalot?'

'No, Hugo, much as though I would like to shift the weight from my back to yours, it isn't good for you to eat too much.'

'Spoilsport,' came the usual reply as we hit the path again.

A young couple came the other way, holding hands and with eyes only for each other.

'Neither of them are country folk,' said Hugo, who had suddenly become an authority on this. 'Look at the clothes, look at the footwear, and look at those sunglasses.'

'Sshh, Hugo, be kind, remember your training. They'll learn and they won't get into harm's way today. It's not as if they were climbing Helvellyn.'

Hugo sniffed. He had decided he wanted to be a rescue dog having read the information on Patterdale mountain rescue the night before. He had become obsessed with being properly equipped for the hills.

'Reminds me of me days being dropped out of aeroplanes with me sled team in Labrador. We had wooden eye protectors with little slits cut into them. Helped with the snow blindness, it did. They didn't have proper dark glasses for dogs.'

'Hugo, you've been reading too much romantic fiction.'

'Helps pass the time, guv.'

We walked on, rounded the base of Silver Crag and looked across at Glenridding.

'There you are, end in sight, Glenridding,' I said to Hugo. 'Going to tell me any more about your Cornish experiences?'

'Suppose I must. I really enjoyed the sanctuary. Carried on with me twelve-paws, of course. Next up we had to make a list of all the persons we'd harmed with our addictions. That were quite easy, there hadn't been too many, and most of the damage I'd done to myself. Top of the list was Zoe, and I've told you about her. Then there was the old soldier. He'd really cared for me, and about me. First proper love, apart from Zoe, since I'd lost me mum. It would all have been different if I'd known then what I know now. Would have been a bit more grateful. Debated whether to put the folk in Sunningdale on the list. Trouble is, I weren't sure who'd done the harming. Rather got the feeling that "Rescue Labrador" was a tick in the box you might say, more done for form than because they loved me. Never felt much love there. Understand what I mean, guv?'

'I do, Hugo. I used to go to an army base once, when I was a young military doctor. A lot of the offices in the headquarters used to have Labradors sprawled across the doorway. I used to wonder whether the Labradors were issued from the stores, or whether they were purchased with the uniform allowance. Always seemed more like a statement of social conformity than genuine dog love. Could have been wrong, though.'

'Got it in one, guv. You was wondering whether they were really, properly loved. We can tell, you know.'

'I know you can. There have been a lot of studies on emotions in dogs and people. Dogs are pretty skilled at recognising and feeling emotion. Not really surprising given the length of time we've evolved together. Now, border collies–'

'Guv, you're going off on one again. I don't need to hear about the intelligence or marathon-running skills of border collies. Bit of a sore point with the rest of us dogs. How often do you see any other breed socialising with border collies? Stand-offish bunch, they are. "Oh, we're the super-intelligent dogs; studies show a border collie can memorise over five hundred different objects . . ."

'Hugo, this isn't like you. Where's your respect, your beliefs?'

'Sorry, guv, but it's difficult when you get a group that does consistently better than other groups in the old Einstein department. Sets them apart from the rest of us "Happy-go-lucky, of course I'll get your pheasant for you," dogs. I just have to work on liking them. It doesn't come naturally, even for me, and I've done a lot with me twelve-paws and philosophy.'

'But, Hugo, look at you. You are an exceptional dog, by any standard. You are one of a handful that can talk. You don't have to feel like that, and what's more, you know how dangerous that line of thinking is. Remember where it takes us.'

'I know, guv, it's the whole instinct versus thinking thing. It seems we have some instincts that aren't very nice. It's why we have this idea that we should "love our neighbour as ourselves". Trouble is, it's hard when they are some super-intelligent border collie, and you know they're so much brighter than you are. I try and like them, but I really have to work at it. It doesn't come naturally. It's frequently one of me meditations.'

'Glad to hear it, Hugo.'

We walked on down and joined the farm track near Blowick. More walkers were out now and it had turned into the typical "Lakeland on a sunny day in the season" walk. Hugo was in his element. Lots of people, all with food, all to be "worked".

He came up to me. 'Where's Booth's, guv?'

'What, you mean the Waitrose of the north? Why?'

'Seem to have cornered the "lunch in the hills" market. Wondered if we could go there?'

'See how your paws feel when we get back to the caravan.'

"'What have you got for us to eat later?'

'Usual stuff, Hugo, you saw what I got in the farm shop.'

'I saw you get enough for the breakfast and lunch we've already had, and even that was short rations, if I may so. Hard to sustain a healthy Labrador on what I've eaten today.'

'Alright, we'll see how I feel when we get back to the caravan.'

'Humph.'

We were just going through Side Farm when I got a text from my brother: "Got in touch with the Standard Poodle Club. They are checking their records and will get back to me. More info when I get it."

Hugo's response was surprisingly downbeat.

'What happens if they do find her, guv? It was a long time ago now, and she must have been really upset when I just disappeared. She might not want to hear from me, let alone see me. She might have created a whole new life for herself. It might bring back all sorts of bad memories. I feel scared at the idea of seeing her.'

'Hold your horses, Hugo. She hasn't been found yet. My brother has only just taken the first steps.'

'I know, guv, but it's really scary. Of course I want to see her, and would love to pick up where we left off, but I know that life isn't like that.'

'Do you want me to call off the search? We don't have to contact her, even if we do find her?'

'No, guv. I'd like to know if she can be found and if she is alright. Can we leave it like that for the moment?'

'Of course, Hugo. Sounds like it's a pretty big problem for you, so let's take it one bit at a time.'

Hugo ambled off, deep in his own thoughts. I could always tell when he was out of sorts because his walk became a sort of four-legged slouch, with his head, ears and tail down. Even his shoulders changed, with his body sagging with each step as if everything was too much effort. I watched him for a while, ambling aimlessly, ignoring passers-by and generally a picture of dejection. I left him to his own thoughts until we approached the road back to Glenridding, when I called him over to me.

'Having a tough time?'

'You know what it's like, guv. You think everything is going along OK and you've got stuff sorted out in your head – oh yes, me head is in a good place today! – and then suddenly something comes along and wham! All your carefully made-up defences just crumble and your head becomes filled with all the bad stuff that you've done and you've had done to you. You just collapse inside and think, is there ever any end to this?'

'My turn to be the therapist, Hugo. It's been a long day, you're tired, you haven't had much to eat, and you've just had a really, really big emotional challenge. It's normal to feel like that. You know what emotional triggers do to us. Now, I am going to be boringly predictable and upbeat. Suppose we go to Keswick on our way back to the caravan? We'll get a chicken biryani takeout and have a quiet night in and an early bed?'

'Suppose so.'

***

Later that evening Hugo became a bit more communicative.

'You can never escape your past, can you, guv?'

'Not the memories, no.'

'Doesn't do any good dwelling on them.'

'No, it doesn't. They are part of what makes you as you are, but they mustn't stop you moving forward. Much better to live in the present and use the lessons you have learned to make the future a better and happier place.'

'Doesn't help when you keep on getting triggers reminding you of the past.'

'That's true. It's why sometimes we have to leave the past behind us and make a new life.'

'Not easy, guv.'

'Not always possible, either, Hugo.'

'Goodnight, guv.'

'Night-night, Hugo.'

I watched him curl himself up in a tight ball in his Labrador-tartan bed. He seemed to go off to sleep straight away, but I knew there would be half an ear cocked for trouble. I got the duvet and fell asleep on the sofa beside him.

Chapter 10

The Drinking Bird

We got up early the next morning and went into Keswick. Hugo had wanted to see Booths; purveyors, in his mind, of lunches on the hill. I left him sitting in the car, watching the comings and goings whilst I went in to get our food.

'Fascinating, guv.'

'What is, Hugo?'

'Different tribe the anorak brigade. Not what I'm used to seeing.'

'We are a long way from London, Hugo.'

'I know, guv. Did you know there are at least three different tribes of people going in and out of the store? There's the locals, there's the trippers, and then there's the folk who are going out on the hills. Fascinating. Different cars, different foods, different clothes, different boots.'

'I know, Hugo, but there is something else about them too.'

'Oh, I noticed that. I was just trying to be politically correct. Not very "cosmopolitan", are they?'

'No, Hugo, definitely not. Do you mind telling me where this is taking us?'

'Addicts is a sort of tribe, guv. Ever thought about it?'

'A bit.'

"Ever seen the drinking bird toy?'

'I have. Used to fascinate me when I was a kid.'

'It's a good model for thinking about addiction.'

'Why?'

'If you watch it, it just sits there, looking at the glass in front of it, and then slowly it leans forward and dips its beak in the water. It stays there for a bit, then goes back upright and stares into space for a long while, and then slowly leans forward and repeats everything again, and again and again. The only thing that stops it is when there is no water in the glass.'

'So why is it a model for addiction?'

'Think about it. When it's upright, it doesn't seem to move. If you're a relative, or "nearest and dearest", you relax. You think, ah, thank goodness, stopped drinking - or, in my case, eating - maybe we can relate again normally? Then, crash! away go your dreams as the head goes down to drink again. It's down there drinking for a while, and then comes back up. But then it's nodding backwards and forwards. It's all over the place. Gradually it settles and you start to let your guard down again. You've been imploring them to stop drinking, taking drugs or overeating, and it looks like you've succeeded, and then your dreams get taken away again.'

'I know what you mean, Hugo, I've seen it a lot. Must be worst for kids. They don't understand. One moment they see their parent sort of OK, and then they're drinking and shouting and there's violence and their world collapses.'

'Exactly, guv, and the worst part is they feel partially responsible. They don't understand that it has got nothing to do with them and everything to do with the addiction. Doesn't matter whether it's alcohol, gambling, food or drugs, it's all about the addict, not those around them.'

'And the other thing is the enabling. Because you carry on loving and supporting the addict, you enable them to continue with their addiction.'

'Right again, guv. Now, where are we going? I've had enough of this for the moment.'

I sorted things out in the car so that Hugo couldn't get at our lunch.

'Typical, you still don't trust me.'

'Do you trust yourself?'

I heard a mumbled, 'Suppose not,' as he twirled around and settled himself down on the back seat. I cracked the window open for him and set off up Borrowdale.

We were lucky enough to find a vacant space in the car park at Rosthwaite and, after locking up, we set off.

'Notice you haven't cleaned your boots for a bit.'

'Could say the same about your paws. Had to clean up after you in the caravan this morning.'

'Didn't think you'd notice.'

'How could I miss it? Anyway, it's not my caravan, we've got to leave it as we found it.'

'You did pack me lunch?'

'Yes. You saw I did.'

'Just checking. Can I have it now?'

'No, we've only just started and it's still early. Apart from water, and possibly the odd treat, you've had your lot until lunchtime. We are stopping to eat in Grange, but you've got Castle Crag to go up before then.'

'I'm not good at heights, guv.'

'You'll be fine. There's no exposure and it is only a steep walk. Anyway, I thought you were the intrepid explorer.'

'In me dreams. Reality is sometimes a bit different.'

'Hugo, you're not telling me you're a bit of a fantasist.'

'Never done anything like this, guv. Don't know how I'll manage.'

'You'll be OK. You've got four-paw-drive and I'll coax you up with a box of treats.'

'Doesn't that make you complicit in me food addiction?'

'This time, Hugo, it makes me a realist. I know the only way I'll get you up Castle Crag is to keep your lunch firmly in my backpack and drip feed you with morsels from the treat box. Otherwise it will be your usual trick of four feet firmly planted on the ground and you moaning, "That's not the way. . ."'

'What is for lunch?'

''Cold chicken biryani.'

'Guv?'

'Yes?'

'I'll go up Everest for that.'

'Thought you might.'

And with that exchange we set off.

I took the low way round to Castle Crag, following the river. It was turning into a warm day and I thought Hugo might like to paddle his paws.

He started grumbling early on. 'How far is this walk?'

'Oh, a few miles.'

'Longer than me normal walk on the Heath?'

'Yes.'

'But I get fed at the end of that.'

'You'll get fed at the end of this one.'

'But it's longer, how am I going to cope?'

'You will.'

'Won't. I'm going back.'

'You don't know the way.'

'Yes, I do.'

'Even so, you may not have noticed, but you've got your long lead on. The extendable one. You go where I go.'

'You did that deliberately.'

'Yep.'

'Guv, you're getting to know me too well.'

'Had to, Hugo. You always think "food".'

'Try not to, but it's hard when I'm away from me normal rituals. I've told you before that food addiction is different. You have to eat less, and the best way of coping is by having a regular stable routine. Haven't got that up here. Scenery is lovely, of course, and there are lots of interesting sniffs, but me routine has changed, and if I don't know when me next meal is coming I think more about food.'

'Want a treat?'

'It would help.'

And with that honour was satisfied for a bit and we wandered on.

'Tell me some more about your time in Cornwall.'

'Anything in particular?'

'I'm interested in the bit where you dogs went through the twelve-paws. I didn't feel very comfortable with the way you did that. Seemed too easy.'

'You forget, guv, just because I can talk doesn't mean we don't have differences. Dogs do better on training than humans. You may have noticed, even if I'm searching for a bin, I'll always come back for the sound of the rattlebox because that contains something to eat. It's embedded in me head. Rattlebox always means a treat. Bin only means potential for a snack that might not be too savoury, if you get me drift. It's a kind of a "bird in the hand beats one in the bush" scenario. What they were doing for us was laying down rules by training. I've told you before that we had very structured days. Food was regular. Training was regular. Exercise was regular. Obedience was instilled. Atmosphere was loving but tough. Perfect for us dogs. We like to know where we stand. You've got to remember, as we've said, that food addiction is different. Stopping eating isn't an option. You have to learn a pattern of eating that's safe.'

'Didn't seem to work too well for you.'

'Yes, well, I'm a bit different, as you might have noticed. Bit of a free spirit.'

'Rather like the other night in London, when we took you for a walk at dusk and you suddenly did the old black Lab merging into the gloom trick.'

'Precisely. But couldn't you smell them?'

'Smell what?'

'The leftover smoked salmon bagels; or, more precisely, as I discovered to my disappointment, the place where the leftover smoked salmon bagels had been but were no more. That's why I went on the hunt.'

'But I still don't understand why the twelve-paws. Why not just the training?'

'Actually, guv, I think it was a bit of an experiment. They were also treating humans with addiction and so they put us all through the same sort of program. Some of us went off after our time there to be therapist dogs, and knowing about it was really helpful.'

'So, you think routine is important?'

'Certain of it. Routine and a stable, supportive pack around you, that's what keeps you out of trouble.'

'Do you think that works for humans?'

'Think so. But you know the addict has got to really want to do something about their addiction for themselves. That's the biggest hurdle. Lots never get there. They can't or won't recognise the need to change. Too difficult or too scary. They cause a lot of damage to the family around them in the process.'

'I've seen that in my practice.'

'What did you see?'

'A range of things. My experience was mostly with alcohol, and I saw anger at loved ones getting drunk, then attempts to talk to them about their drinking, and failure, generally, to get anywhere with that. And then despair that things would ever change for the better. It was hard for children, as we've discussed. They can't understand what's going on. They see sudden mood swings and occasional violence that seems to come out of nowhere and it's confusing and frightening for them.'

'Did you see anything else?'

'Yes. Shame featured in it. The family felt ashamed of the behaviour of their loved one. They felt rejected too. It was as if the alcohol mattered more than the relationship and their love. What was worse, was that they came to believe what they were told, which was that they had done something wrong and the drinking was the response. Very confusing and very destructive. Sometimes they would get suckered in to drinking with their loved one when they didn't really want to. They did it to keep them company and try and control their loved one's drinking that way.'

'That never works,' said Hugo. 'It just reinforces the addiction and makes them feel they are being watched and controlled. Mark you, you see that sometimes with the owners of food-addicted dogs. Fat dog, fat owner. Hard to know who has the problem sometimes.'

By now we were well up Lingy Bank on our way to the Old Quarry Path.

Hugo decided to change the subject. 'Don't think much to this mountaineering, guv. I'm having difficulty walking and talking at the same time.'

'Hugo, you old layabout, this is no worse than walking up to Hampstead Heath, and you don't normally protest over that.'

'You don't have to cast aspersions. Me, a layabout? I'll have you know I'm a properly registered therapist Labrador. It's just that nobody mentioned when I signed up for me training that I'd have to do it on an empty stomach, halfway up a mountain, after hours of gruelling walking.'

'Hugo, you're incorrigible. Firstly, we've been only walking for about half an hour; secondly, it's not gruelling; and finally, what did you think your therapy sessions were going to be like?'

'Well, personally I thought I would be curled up in a comfy chair with a bowl of treats on the table and me client stretched out on a couch telling me stuff.'

'Hugo, you know perfectly well you were never going to be some Labrador version of Sigmund Freud. Anyway, you told me your therapy model was you talked and your client listened. And, what is more, you weren't giving a therapy session just then, we were comparing notes. And–'

'I know. if I'm getting out of breath it's because I eat too much and don't take enough exercise.'

'Exactly.'

'I asked you to avoid that word.'

'Sorry.'

We walked on up to the Old Quarry Path in silence, each lost in thought.

After a while, 'Guv?'

'Yes?'

'Where are we going?'

'Right up Castle Crag.'

'Up there?'

'Yes.'

'It's enormously steep. I can't do that.'

We had reached the point where the little path up to the top veered off the Quarry Road. Hugo had stopped, sat down, and was looking in disbelief at our little climb.

'You expect me to go up there?'

'Yes.'

'Not a chance.'

'Why not?'

'For a start, I haven't got the energy; for seconds, it's already making me wobbly; and for thirds, I'm hungry.'

'I thought you were the intrepid adventurer who jumped out of low-flying aeroplanes with his trusty sled team to go on rescues across the Labrador winter wilderness?'

'I was young and foolhardy then.'

'You're going up.'

'No, I'm not.'

'You are, because I've got the rations and you'll feel so much better when you've done it. Besides which, we both need to work off what we have already eaten.'

'Guv, I've got a terrible wobble.'

'Hugo, old lad, believe me, you'll cope with this just fine. I'll keep you on your lead. You're much closer to the ground than I am, you've got four-paw-drive, as well you know, and you can just follow on where I put my feet.'

We set off. I could hear the occasional sharp intakes of breath and, 'I need food. I'm also a comfort eater,' but we made progress upwards until we came to the spoil heap.

'It feels awfully open, guv. Lots of fresh air. I don't like the way things slip under me paws.'

'One step at a time, Hugo. Watch where you put your feet. Say to yourself, "I can do it," and remember, when we get to the top, we will have a sit down and a snack.'

'What sort of a snack?'

'A mouthful of chicken biryani sort of a snack.'

With that Hugo's resolve stiffened. He took the lead, positively tugging me up the last few feet to the top. We sat down and looked back up Borrowdale.

'Never seen anything like this before, guv.'

'I think it's very special. It's one of my favourite places in the world.'

'Travelled much?'

'Enough to know that this valley is a little corner of paradise. It produces a sort of deep calm. I know few things better than coming out here with a good friend, on a long walk. Rather like today.'

'Interesting isn't it, guv, the way walking and talking go together. It's a bit funny when you write the conversations down, because they seem to jump around a bit, but you actually cover a lot of ground and it doesn't half make you feel better.'

'Absolutely, Hugo. I thought of setting up a therapy clinic once, where we'd bring people from the cities up to the hills for a week and just make them walk and talk. Healthy for everybody, I thought. You've given me an idea. Perhaps we could do it with a bunch of therapist Labradors. We'd have to get the Labradors used to the mountains first, of course. Can't have them going all snowflake.'

'Am I ever going to live this down, guv?'

'Hugo, it's allowed. If you'd never experienced this before you've done really well. Castle Crag is a good introduction because it's an easy walk. We'll have you enjoying the wide, open spaces of Cat Bells soon. You'll love it. Oh, and the other thing, what happens on a walk stays on a walk. I won't tell anybody.'

'What about your book?'

'You get to benefit from the royalties if it's published.'

'Humph, that's a pretty high price to pay for loss of me dignity. I'll hold you to the blue lobster.'

'Deal.'

We sat for a while in the sun, enjoying the view.

Hugo tried demanding more chicken biryani. 'Just one more mouthful, for the road, guv?'

'No, you're having the rest for your lunch.'

We set off again.

'Cor, did we really come up this? Looks awfully steep going down!'

'We did. Just keep your weight evenly on your paws and you'll be fine.'

And down we went, Hugo gaining in confidence with every step.

We picked up the Quarry Road again and carried on to Grange. Hugo was in his element now. New-found confidence from his climb and descent – the confidence that comes from having conquered some of your demons – and that general wonderful feeling that comes from being outside on a beautiful day in beautiful scenery. He implored any passers-by with his best winning ways for any scraps they might have to offer, and still managed a very polite tail wag on the rare occasions when he was turned down. He was one happy Labrador.

'Guv?'

'Yes, Hugo?'

'I like it here. Can we come again?'

''Whenever we can find time and the caravan is free.'

'Did you mean that about walking and talking?'

'I think it's a very good idea. It could fit in with you being a therapist dog very well. It would keep you fit, and save on the upkeep of a therapist's couch.'

'I did have this fantasy of being a bit Freud-like.'

'Go for the insight not for the image. You remember, see things as they really are.'

'Can we talk about addiction again?'

'Of course, but let's have some ground rules. Are you in therapist mode or are we just having a chat?'

'Just having a chat.'

'OK.'

'I want to talk to you about living with an addict.'

'Difficult and painful.'

'How do you see it?'

'With you, a bit of a trial sometimes. I can never let my guard down. I have to constantly check that anything edible is out of your way. And it would be nice sometimes to think that you really loved us, rather than getting that sinking feeling that you only love us because we provide your grub.'

'I do love you all, guv, particularly 'Er Ladyship, her children and the little people. Even put up with you.'

'Thank you, Hugo.'

'Don't mention it. But what did your patients tell you about living with an addict?'

'That it's very, very hard. In the early stages, when you don't know they're an addict, you wonder where the mood swings come from. When the diagnosis is made your first thoughts are, great, now someone is going to treat them and it's all going to get better; but, after a while, you learn that isn't the case.

'You find that it's very hard to get treatment for them; that even if you do, a lot of the abnormal behaviours continue even though they may have temporarily stopped overeating or drinking, or whatever it is they are addicted to. Look at yourself. Even when we keep you on the straight and narrow you are always thinking about food. You may not be a barrel, and you may not be bingeing, but food is uppermost in your mind. You are like an alcoholic thinking "drink".

'I'm afraid you're right.'

'My patients also told me that it's very difficult to work out what you should be doing, thinking or feeling. Your world becomes topsy-turvy. The funny thing is, you don't realise how topsy-turvy the world is, because you've gradually become used to it. The rows, the binges and everything are wrong, but they're part of the scene. When it's your nearest and dearest you want to help them, and you try every which way, but slowly and surely you get affected by it and you lose track of reality.'

'Gradually, very gradually, you come to the understanding that you cannot help them. You come to realise that the addict is on their own. Until they recognise their problem and decide that they alone are going to do something about it there is no support the family, or pack, can offer. That is heart-breaking.

'Addicts don't mean to do it, guv.'

'I know. Another problem for kids is that adults think a kid has the same emotional development as they have. It gets forgotten that people don't have an emotional development any older than they are, and that often, in an addict's family, they have no concept of what actually is normal. Now, you are an insightful addict, how do you see it?'

'A lot of the time I don't really see it at all, guv. I know I'll always be an addict, and I have difficulty controlling me urges, as you've noticed, but I understand why I'm an addict, and I know the importance of living a stable life and talking about things when I start to have one of me wobbles. Before, I would just follow me addiction, but I've learnt about that now, and I use me friends and me pack for help and support. A lot of the time, when you and I are together, it's just a game that I play; but I know the serious problem is never very far away. The trouble is, even when I'm not bingeing, it takes so much of my effort to stay on the straight and narrow that I don't have much time to think of anybody else – even with me famous Labrador love and affection. "Once an addict, always an addict," as they say. Me training is very important, and I have to keep to this daily routine, and I have to keep reminding myself of how to cope. That's why I do the mindfulness bit every day, but it's hard work, very hard work.'

'How do you cope with statements like "Addicts always lie"?'

'It's sadly true. It is less when we have gained control of our addiction, because we know that lying takes us down the slippery path again, but we are always at risk. I know it's very destructive in relationships. Had a client once who used to silently rage that he could never trust his partner. Everything would seem normal and happy for a bit, he'd let his guard down and think everything was alright, and then wham! it would all change again. I suppose I'm a dreadful dog to live with.'

'Sometimes, but by no means always.'

'Don't mean to be, guv,' said Hugo, disconsolately.

'I know, Hugo, and you know how much we love you.'

By this time, we'd reached Grange. We found an outside table at a little café by the side of the road. I filled Hugo's collapsible bowl with water and gave him the rest of his chicken biryani. I went in search of a menu, while Hugo lay in the shade.

'Can I have some of that?'

'Hugo, do you ever stop trying?'

'No, guv. I think food. Simple as that. Surely you've sussed it by now?'

'I have, but it does get a bit tiresome. Anyway, your treat today was cold chicken biryani. I know it's hard, but mine is a couple of toasted sandwiches.'

'Bloody capitalist exploiting the workers.'

'Since when have you been a worker?'

'Since I read "Das Kapital".'

'You're having me on.'

'Might be.'

We sat, me enjoying the sun. My toasted sandwiches came and I got to eat them, despite the usual protests. Eventually I got up and paid the bill. Hugo was still sprawled out watching the world go by.

'Come on, time to move.'

'Must we? It's nice here in the shade.'

'Yes.'

'Where are we going?'

'Back to Rosthwaite.'

'That's miles.'

'Rubbish. It's two miles back along the river.'

'So we're not going back up Castle Crag?'

'No.'

'Can we do some rock climbing?'

'Easy, tiger, it's not really a Labrador sport.'

'I've been reading about the north face of the Eiger.'

'You're fantasising again. They'd have to haul you up.'

'Well, it'd take me thoughts off tea.'

We set off again, making for the trees by the side of the river. Hugo was still full of beans and happily chased into the river and generally behaved more like a Lab than I had seen for some time. I left him to his own devices. In his own inimitable way, he did actually work as a therapist Labrador. There really was a lot of life experience in the old boy, and his roguish charm did much to remove the irritation of his constant food drive. Walking with him had done me a power of good, principally because he was so funny – although I was not sure that this was always his intent. Eventually, as the trees gave way to grass, he came back to join me and I had to put him back on his lead.

'Don't like this, guv.'

'I know, Hugo, but it's the rule when there are sheep around.'

'But I'm not interested in chasing them. That's a job for the border collies.'

'It's still the rule, and it's designed to keep you safe as

much as the sheep.'

'What's for tea?'

'I am planning a treat. The famous Yew Tree Farm Tea Room is at the end of our walk. Thought we might go in there.

'Do they do northern teas? Can I have some fruit cake, and a slice of cheese?'

'Sponge cake, yes; slice of cheese, maybe; fruit cake, no. You know it isn't good for you.'

And so we went and had tea in Rosthwaite. Hugo had his piece of cake. I had tea in a half-pint mug. And we both had that glow that comes from a pleasant day out with a little bit of exercise. We went back to the car and drove home to the caravan. Hugo slept well that night and the next morning we packed up and drove back down to London.

As we were passing the turn off for the M65, Hugo perked up.

'You like social history. Ever hear of the Rawtenstall Clinic for Stray Dogs?'

'No.'

'Founded by one of the Queen's corgis it were. They used to have a real problem with food addiction in the mongrels round there. It were on account of all the dropped Bury black pudding, mushy peas, tripe, Eccles cakes and so on. Drove the dogs wild. Set the clinic up in an old weaving shed. We must go there one day and see if it's still running.'

'You're having me on again.'

'I'm not, the lurcher told me. Very reliable dogs lurchers.'

'I always thought they were a bit shady.'

'There you go, exhibiting your prejudices again.'

'Sorry, Hugo.'

'Tell you another thing.'

'Yes, Hugo.'

'Up here was the home of a very famous extinct dog breed, the Morecombe Bay shrimp hound.'

'You're having me on again!'

'No, I'm not. Heard about it on the radio once. It was one of those spoken series, you should try and find it. Uncle Mort in the North Country.'

'I'll look out for it, Hugo. The Morecombe Bay shrimp hound. It's a wonderful image.'

On the way back, my brother phoned to say no news about Zoe, but he was still on the case.

Hugo went very quiet in the back, lost in his thoughts.

Chapter 11

Little Devils

I didn't see Hugo for quite some time after that. I went off to visit my family and Hugo settled back into life with his mistress. When I got back he was less than amused.

'Morning. Blowing in, are we?'

'Not quite the greeting I expected, Hugo.'

'Didn't expect you to be away this long. Her indoors is busy but she always finds time for me. At least I can rely on her not skiving off and forgetting about me. She loves me. I do not like bits of me pack just wandering off. I feel insecure. Me quality of life declines when that happens and I've told you how important having a good pack around me is. Me mistress gets that, she saved me, and she never forgets how much I need saving. It's called unconditional love, as you may remember.'

'OK, Hugo, I feel truly put back in my box. I thought you got to spend a bit more of your time chilling out with your mates at Auntie Elly's when I was away?'

'I do. Me Aunty Elly is wonderful and looks after me so well. It's also nice to see a different set of friends but, you know what it's like, after a while you start to think of home and your pack.'

'But you have clients to see, other dogs and people to look after?'

'Doesn't make up for it. I've had a terrible time since you've been away. Diagnosed with gallstones, but you know about that, and gawd knows what else. Had me diet changed to hypoallergenic, treats included, and to cap it all they've told me I got pernicious anaemia. Pernicious anaemia, me! Got the indignity of Vitamin B12 shots every week and, by the way, that's your job now you're back. On top of everything else, Uncle Herriot–'

'Who is Uncle Herriot?'

'Me vet. Uncle Herriot is taking an unnatural interest in me bottom. Got to do something about stopping me rubbing me backside he says.'

'I have to tell you, Hugo, you're looking in better condition than when I last saw you. Something must be working.'

'Do you know what's bothering me?'

'No.'

'That chicken biryani I had in the Lakes. Could be me last one, ever.'

'I'm sure it won't be. Now why don't I go and change and we'll go up to the Heath.'

'Rather go to Bigwood.'

'I'd rather go to the Heath.'

'Force Majeure, is it?'

'Yes.'

'Better bring the rattlebox then or I'll go walkabout.'

'You are out of sorts.'

Hugo grunted.

We wandered up to the Heath. Hugo cheerfully splashed

through the various little streams, and generally behaved like a normal Labrador.

'So, what have you been up to?'

'Seeing the family.'

'Thought I was family?'

'You are.'

'What you going away for, then?'

'I have other family, Hugo.'

'Told you, it's important to keep your pack around you, aren't we all enough for you?'

'You have other family too, Hugo. You really should look Ethel up one day.'

'Humph, you could put that the other way round. She's never bothered to look for me.'

'Hugo, did you miss me?'

'Dunno about that . . . might have.'

And with that he was gone again, rootling round benches the other side of the field. I walked on for a bit, expecting him to reappear, but he had gone to ground, I couldn't see him. I waited a bit longer and then whistled. No response. I whistled again. Still no response. I shook the rattlebox containing his treats. In a flash, Hugo was beside me.

'There you are, it works.'

'What are you talking about, Hugo?'

'I've trained you to the rattlebox. Now you're going to have to give me a treat because you think you are obligated because I've come back.'

'And if I don't?'

'Won't come back until I want to, and then you'll really worry.'

'This is blackmail, Hugo.'

'It's better than the alternative.'

I gave him a treat and we wandered on.

'Do you ever think about behaviour, guv?'

'What, as in you can sometimes be a very tiresome Labrador who goes walkabout and is only retrieved by his rattlebox and a treat?'

'I'm hurt.'

'No, you're not.'

'You don't understand. You're thinking of the good boy, bad boy type of behaviour. Think of behaviour as a learned response to a stimulus. What really happens is that I feel in need of a treat. So, I go on a bit of a stroll on me own, knowing that you'll get worried after a bit and blow your whistle and shake me rattlebox. I oblige you by emerging from the undergrowth and thundering across the field to get a pat and a tasty morsel. I get what I wanted all along. You get a sense of relief that I'm back, and a mild degree of irritation that I don't hang around you. You'll have to learn to deal with that, you know.'

'You're a rogue.'

'No, I'm not. I'm a very insightful therapist Labrador. There's a world of difference.'

'I still think you're a rogue.'

'There you go again, persisting in a false belief simply because it agrees with your prejudices. Some people call it lazy thinking, but it's not really thinking at all, it's just lazy. Remember, you've got to try and see things as they really are.'

'Explain yourself.'

'I've just explained it, but you don't get it, do you? Basically, you look at a dog as a sort of cuddly, loveable, loving, trainable robot. You give me food, take me for a walk, and reward me for doing things you want me to do. You've been brought up by other dog owners to think that's how it works. But there is an alternative explanation.'

'Oh yes?'

'Look at it from my point of view. All animals, humans included, like the easy life. They want stuff to just happen. Being a dog, I like food, regular exercise and playing with me mates. I also like regular treats. Makes me feel warm inside and well disposed towards you. How do I get them? Easy! Wander off when you're nice and comfortable on your walk; then induce a little bit of panic, shake you out of your comfort zone, get you a bit worried about me. You mutter under your breath, "Where's that bloody Labrador now?" You shake the rattlebox, and I come charging up with a cheesy grin on me face, wag me tail, get me treat. Manipulate you every time.

'Now, part of the problem for you is you spend too much of your time doing, not thinking. I do the opposite. I spend most of me life sleeping and thinking. Being a food addict, I mostly think about how I get food. If I were a border collie, I would mostly think about sheep. Problem about that is that it sends you to sleep. Can you imagine? There you are, on your bed after a hard day out, reflecting on your accomplishments. Wow, you think, I penned 500 sheep today. Or was one missing? So you conjures up your mental image and start counting. Next thing, bang! you're out cold. Border collies may be the Einsteins of the dog world, but they also sleep the most. Stands to reason. It's the sheep.'

By this time my sides were aching with laughter. Hugo was offended, and wandered off muttering about there being no point in casting pearls before swine, and there's none so blind as won't see.

I shook his rattlebox. In a flash he was back beside me.

'Pavlovian moment?'

Hugo looked embarrassed. 'Suppose so,' he said grudgingly. 'Doesn't mean I can't still manipulate you, though.'

We walked on for a bit.

'Which bit of your family did you go and see?'

'My daughter in Scotland.'

'Where's me haggis, then?'

'No haggis I'm afraid, Hugo.'

'No haggis! I suppose you're going to tell me they were out of season. Well, what about shortbread, oatcake, tablet, a bridie, a buttery, a deep-fried Mars Bar?'

Hugo had clearly been doing his homework, as he'd worked his way through the less healthy options of Scottish fare.

'None of those, I'm afraid.'

'Well, what then?'

The tone was getting grumpy.

'Nothing.'

'Nothing?'

'Nothing, but I did get an invitation.'

'Oh yeah?'

'For you to come up next time. That way you get to see a new bit of country, and you can try out some new foods as a treat when you get there.'

'Accommodation any good?'

'You'll have to share it with a cat.'

'Not my friend Marmalade?'

'No, a black cat with attitude and sharp claws. It will be best behaviour time.'

'Guv?'

'Yes.'

'How is it that every cloud has a leaden lining when I'm with you?'

'You're the therapist, you tell me.'

Hugo grunted. 'Not in the mood for therapy anymore,' he said, and ambled off into the undergrowth again.

Sensing that the morning was not going well I decided to give my brother a call to see whether there was any progress on finding Zoe.

'Still on the case, bro,' he said. 'I tried the art school, who remembered having a standard poodle as a life model. They're checking their records for the owner's details. I hope to hear by the end of the week.'

I decided to wait on telling Hugo until I had something definite to say. We walked on to the upper end of the Heath Extension, where Hugo came to join me. I put his lead on.

'I can be trusted, you know.'

'Your mistress would kill me if anything happened to you.'

'I dunno. Trusted to be a therapist but not to cross the road.'

'That's the way the cookie crumbles, Hugo. You should know yourself well enough to realise what would happen if you saw someone drop a sandwich on the other side of the road.'

'You're forgetting what happened to me brother. I always keep a look out.'

'You're still going on your lead.'

'Control freak.'

I let him off as we walked up onto Sandy Heath. Still out of sorts, he ambled off to a safe distance where we could both keep an eye on each other.

Sandy Heath was originally laid down as a sandbank of a huge river that flowed from the west of England to the east. If you look carefully you can find particles of granite from Dartmoor and rounded pebbles of flint from Wessex. There is always a story to be seen if you keep your eyes open. Later on, the sand and gravel was dug out for all sorts of construction projects, including the London end of the Midland railway. The area is now reforested, but full of dips and ponds. I looked around whilst Hugo went to watch the ducks. Eventually we met up.

'What you been up to?'

'A bit of geologising, how about you?'

'Duck-watching. I like ducks, as you know. Sometimes I wish I was one.'

'It's a recurring theme of yours, why?'

'Freedom, I think. I get quite frustrated as a dog sometimes.'

'Why?'

'Burden of expectation. All me humans want me to be a good boy and be predictable. Wag me tail when you get up in the morning. Wag me tail when you give me breakfast – always late, by the way. Wag me tail when you take me for a walk. Wag me tail when you give me my second breakfast, and so it goes on. No room for madness or creativity. What do you think I'm thinking about when you see me laying on me day-bed?'

'Food.'

'There you go, lazy thinking. Just because I am a food addict, in some sort of recovery, you think I am thinking about food all the time. You 'ave no evidence for your comment.'

'Well, aren't you?'

'No.'

'Well, what then?'

'The joys of being a duck.'

'And they are?'

'The ability to see you coming and have the option to sit there looking cute and decorative, or fly off to a pond the other side of the road without having to sit and have me lead put on. Mark you, they are also good at sitting there all serene whilst paddling like fury underneath. Can be masters of disguise.'

'You are in a bad way this morning. Get out of the wrong side of the bed?'

''Can't do that, too high on three sides. There's only one way in and out, as you well know. Another bit of control.'

'What's upset you?'

'I dunno. Fed up with me guts not being right. Fed up with me diet restriction. Fed up with having to have B12 injections. Don't get me wrong, I appreciate all the care, but I'm just fed up with not being normal. Then you gallivanted off to the other bit of your pack. Didn't like that, although I understand. Don't fancy a cuddle, do you?'

So we found place to sit and I put my arm around him. Hugo leant against me and watched the ducks on the pond. Time went by.

'Time to go, guv, I'm getting stiff. I could murder a chicken biryani.'

'I'll see what I can do.'

Tucked away in Willesden is a curry house renowned for its biryani. I had been debating with myself whether to order a takeaway for some time. I rang my friend.

'He's really low this morning.'

'I noticed. I am quite worried.'

'How about a treat for him? I thought we could organise a takeaway from the place I told you about, the one in Willesden?'

'I'll get on to it now. Lunchtime today? He needs cheering up.'

'I agree. But I'm a bit concerned we might be enabling him. He's been quite good for a while. Lots of grumbles, but no actual binges. I've not seen him this low before, though. I expect it's been caused by his gut problems. There is some evidence that low mood and depression is linked to inflammation.'

'We have a choice. Treat or no treat. If he cheers up and sticks with his diet nothing has been lost. If he starts bingeing again, we will have made a mistake. But I'm afraid he's going to comfort eat given half a chance if we do nothing. Anyway, quite fancy a biryani myself.'

That being settled, Hugo and I walked home. By the time we got there the takeaway had arrived.

Hugo was delighted. 'Best chicken biryani I've had for a long time. What's for afters?' he asked.

'Nothing.'

'Some people have no feelings. I could murder a sticky toffee pudding with lashings of Bird's custard and skin. Cartmel sticky toffee pudding would be best.'

My friend and I looked at each other. When it came to food, Hugo was never satisfied.

After lunch, my friend had to go in to central London. Hugo and I went along for the ride and she dropped us off by St James's Park.

We crossed the Mall into the park and wandered down to see the ducks. These had always been a favourite of mine, ever since my grandfather brought me to see them as a small boy. Grandma would put together a small brown paper bag of stale bread for us, and Grandpa would take my hand

and, like Hugo on his lead, take me over the Mall and into the park. We would walk down to the old iron suspension bridge, now long gone, and feed the waterfowl from where there were little coloured pictures of the different types of ducks. Later I would learn that ducks didn't thrive on bread, but that was ten years further on, and around the time when, as a medical student at the old Charing Cross Hospital, one of my professors would bring us and we would sit in a circle of deckchairs for a tutorial where my grandfather had taken me those years before. Like Hugo, I was lost in memory.

Hugo and I walked on in silence, each deep in our own thoughts. Without realising we had walked down to the Guards Memorial, following the route I used to take all those years before. We stood there for a while in contemplation, and then, without thinking, set off towards Jermyn Street. I was keen to see whether the shop where Grandpa had always bought his cheese still existed. Long before we got there I knew that it did, for, all of a sudden, Hugo's nose came up and a sense of purpose came into his stride. This gave me a dilemma, as I could imagine the turmoil in Hugo's mind if I was to leave him outside a cheese shop – and this one in particular.

'Hugo.'

'Yes, guv?'

'This is not a good idea. I'm leading you towards temptation.'

Hugo switched into therapist mode. 'Explain yourself, guv.'

'We both know we are headed towards a wonderful cheese shop. I would be tempted to buy some, and you would be overwhelmingly tempted to steal some. It isn't fair of me.'

'Well thought through, guv, that sounds like a triumph of head over heart.'

'For me, but how about you?'

'Guv, I'm already struggling. I love cheese, any cheese, the smellier the better. Right now, all me training is failing. I'm thinking cheese, I'm following cheese.'

With that he was gone, to the full extent of his lead. It was pitiable. Ribbons of drool fell from his mouth to the pavement, sobs engulfed him, and he looked at me with pleading eyes.

'Guv, if you don't take me away I'm lost. Me addiction has me again, all I can think of is food. I'm having a relapse, guv, help me.'

I knelt down to give him a cuddle and shortened his lead to keep him right beside me. I then hailed a passing taxi to take us home. Hugo looked out as we turned into Piccadilly Circus and then up Regent Street. He groaned as we caught the scent of a curry from Veeraswamy's, and sobbed as we passed the Apple store.

'Guv,' he said, 'please, please can I have some food, any food?'

'You know the answer to that, Hugo, you've got to conquer this.'

'I can't, guv, the cravings are too strong.'

'Hang in there, Hugo, we'll be home soon and you can have a little of your normal food.'

'It won't work, guv, I need flavour. Camembert, bistecca alla Fiorentina, more chicken biryani.'

'Not this time, Hugo,' I said. 'You and I are going to have a serious chat with your mistress about how you can be helped.'

Silently I cursed myself for taking him near Jermyn Street and precipitating a crisis.

'Guv, food addiction is terrible.'

'I know, Hugo.'

'You don't know the half of it. With most addictions, like we've said, you can stop taking what it is you're addicted to, you might have some withdrawal symptoms and need a bit of help and support then but food is different. I've got to keep eating to keep body and soul together, the problem is I just don't know where to stop. Guv, help!' And with that Hugo sobbed uncontrollably.

At the next lights the cabbie slid his partition back. 'You alright in the back there?'

'Not really. This Lab has got a really serious food addiction and he's having a relapse.'

'It happens,' said the cabbie, uncharitably I thought. In my head I thought I could do without any glimpses of the bleeding obvious. Truth was, I was very worried and completely out of my depth in knowing how to handle Hugo.

'Knew a guide dog like that once, used to snaffle fruit off a barrow as she was passing with her owner. Had it down to a fine art, like a magician's sleight of hand it were. One moment there's a Golden Delicious there, next moment there's a sideways snaffle and a golden retriever with a bulge in her mouth and a look of sweet innocence on her face. Barrow boys used to love her. Always arranged fruit for her when they saw her coming.'

Hugo groaned again. The thought of a fruit-laden barrow was too much for him, and as images of paw paws and mangoes flashed in front of his eyes, his groans grew more frequent and his sobs more convulsive.

I phoned his mistress and arranged to meet her at the vet's. The taxi seemed to take forever, Hugo's groans became more intense, and I became more worried about him. Eventually we arrived and, keeping a firm hold on Hugo, I paid the cabbie. Hugo walked in, dejectedly.

'Go straight through,' said the receptionist as the vet appeared.

And that's when it happened. I was just passing Hugo's lead to the vet so that he could have a better look at him when the door opened and another patient came in. In a flash, Hugo was gone, through the still open outer door of the surgery, racing down the parade of shops in search of a fix of food. It was too late to see precisely where he had gone, but I heard the commotion at Cracking Cakes from a hundred yards away. Arriving, the place was in chaos. I could see that Hugo had made straight for the real delicacies and was just finishing, what had been, a very fine dark chocolate birthday cake. He looked at me with pleading eyes.

'I couldn't 'elp it, guv, I needed flavour, I was completely out of control. I've done it now, 'aven't I? It will be like me brother Fred on his chocolate suggestives!'

'Maybe not, Hugo,' said his mistress, who had just arrived and was trying to keep his spirits up. 'We'll do everything we can to help you.'

I carried him back to the vet and explained the situation.

'We may be lucky,' said the vet. 'We've got him early, but he has had a lot of chocolate, and plain chocolate at that. I must tell you he may not survive.'

Hugo groaned as he overheard this. 'Fred!' he called out. 'Why didn't I remember what happened to you?' And he sobbed in remorse as the first wave of sickness convulsed him.

'We'll have to give him an emetic,' said the vet. 'We want him to be sick, and we need to get charcoal biscuits into him.'

'I hate charcoal biscuits!' howled Hugo.

'It's for your own good!' we said, in unison.

'I hate those words!' howled Hugo, as the effects of the chocolate hit him again.

'You need to leave now,' said the vet. 'I have to set up a drip and bring down his pulse rate. It will be touch and go for the next seventy-two hours.'

Hugo howled remorsefully again, 'Oh Fred, why didn't I remember what happened to you?'

'Go, now,' repeated the vet. 'We will look after him.'

And with that, and with heavy hearts and several backward glances, we left Hugo to the tender hands of the vet and an uncertain future.

My phone rang. It was my brother. 'I've found Zoe.'

Chapter 12

Treachery and Crisis

Hugo hovered between life and death for several days. To calm his racing heart, he was deeply sedated, and he drifted in and out of dreams.

In one dream he was in his mistress's beloved Prague. Communist era. Winter. Smuggled into the embassy in the diplomatic bag. The station chief signed to him to be quiet as they made for the secure room. Swept every hour for bugs and built inside a steel cage, the chief waited for the heavy steel door to swing shut and lock before he spoke.

'It's the big one, Hugo, old boy. That's why we sent for you. I've lost two good men already, which is why M sanctioned the use of a black Labrador. Someone in our system is betraying us. We don't think the Czech and Russian secret services know about our "Black-Lab" program, although they know all about the 00s. That way the KGB and StB run around looking for glamorous spies whilst the really dangerous stuff is done by you Labradors. You are to make a pick up in the arcade at the corner of Malé Námésti and Staromêstské Námésti. It's scheduled for ten thirty tonight, which should leave enough time for you to get out of Prague before dawn.

If you are caught, the secret police, the StB, won't bother to interrogate you. They don't know you can talk. They will probably just shoot you – unless someone wants a trophy pet.

Hugo nodded. 'Hmm, not far from the StB headquarters, nothing like hiding in plain sight. Usual magnetic canister on the collar trick, chief?'

'Yes. You will carry one to the drop to exchange. Your box will only release when he has put his box on. The man you are giving it to thinks it contains information for him. It doesn't. It will release a drug that will permanently obliterate his memory of the last forty-eight hours. That way he will forget about you and the details of what he has been doing.'

'Roger that,' Hugo said, tersely. 'Moscow rules?'

'You've been reading too much Le Carré. One long claw scratch on the wall behind the third pillar of the arcade to show you made the pick-up. After that you have ten days to make it over the border. If you don't get there, we will assume you haven't made it and the self-destruct on your collar will activate.'

'Thank you for the vote of confidence,' said Hugo, sarcastically. 'Remind me to bring my own collar next time. I hate these things of yours that go bang. Thank goodness the last one didn't work!'

'How are you going to get out, Hugo?'

'I'll take care of that. Best you don't know.' And with that Hugo started to leave.

'One last thing . . .' said the chief.

'Yes?'

'There's a new type of trdelnik out on the streets, with Nutella. For God's sake stay off it.'

'Do me best,' said Hugo cheerily, thinking how the west was slowly seeping through the Iron Curtain if they now had Nutella. He slipped out through the dog flap, cunningly concealed as an antique coffer, into the embassy kitchen.

***

Later that day, after a siesta in a brief shaft of winter sunlight in one of the reception rooms, Hugo returned to get equipped for his mission. The chief fitted two small curved containers to his collar. 'Any trouble, old boy, and the second container will dispense dog treats laced with rapidly acting tranquilliser. All you have to do is woof twice, softly, for them to drop out.'

'Thanks,' said Hugo. 'I'm just going to think over the arrangements for the drop again, and as soon as it's dark I'll leave.'

'That will give you hours to spare,' said the chief.

'Don't worry about it,' said Hugo. 'I have a plan.' And I'm not telling you, he thought. He always preferred to keep the essentials of his tradecraft close to his chest.

Around teatime he looked out of the window into the embassy garden. He wished he could go out, but the garden was overlooked by the castle above and he had to assume there would be watchers. A quiet meow disturbed him. The ambassador's cat was looking at him from the other side of the room.

'Morning 007,' he said with a sneer. 'Off on a mission again? Oh, I forgot, Labradors don't get a licence to kill.'

Hugo looked at him irritably. He'd met this cat before. Never quite trusted him.

'That's right, and the only licence you get is to kill mice. Anyway, came out for a short holiday; you know what they say, a change is as good as a rest.'

'Humph,' said the cat. 'More likely you got banished because of your appetite.' And, with that parting shot, he went through the cat flap into the garden.

Hugo tried to settle but couldn't. The cat had disturbed him, and he was concerned about how much it might know. To distract himself he followed its scent back through the embassy until he found the cat food bowl, which he emptied in a couple of gulps. He smiled to himself. It was almost a pity he wasn't going to be around to hear the anguished meow when the cat discovered his bowl was empty. What made it even better was the realisation that some of the rations in the diplomatic bag that he'd eaten had actually been cat food. That'll teach him to mock me, thought Hugo, no western grub until the next bag comes. What was it Marmalade called stuck-up cats? Feline poodles. He had a point.

After his snack, Hugo returned to the embassy kitchen, where he spent so much time getting in the way of the chef that he finally relented and cooked him an enormous steak. Another siesta, and he was ready. The chef led him down the stairs to the wine cellar. Behind one of the racks at the back of the cellar was a concealed door. Hugo sniffed and checked carefully. The cobwebs and dust showed that it hadn't been disturbed for some time. The chef opened the door, revealing the entrance to a tunnel. Hugo padded off, making no sound as the door was closed behind him. Unseen in the cellar darkness, two green eyes watched the whole of the proceedings. Satisfied that Hugo had gone, the cat quietly stole away.

At first, the tunnel headed down, but then curled round and then started going uphill. It ended underneath a grating. Hugo stopped and sniffed. Behind him were smells of damp earth; but on the other side of the grating he detected the persistent smell of communist Prague in the winter – fog, burning soft coal, roasted chestnuts, drains and a tinge of fear. He paused. He sniffed again. It didn't feel right, yet he couldn't quite put his paw on it. Oh well, here goes, he thought, and he quietly slid the grating aside and stepped into Snēmovni in the Mala Strana, the Lesser Town.

All his senses were alert. Something still felt wrong. He padded on quietly, heading towards the Wallenstein Palace. A tram rumbled past, its occupants illuminated against the surrounding darkness. Hugo shivered and withdrew further into the shadows. He had just entered Tomášská when he heard a shout: 'Zustan!' – 'Stay!' – and a couple of flashlights came on. Hugo could dimly see two policemen, one with a large Doberman on a lead. He thought quickly. Best to run and hope they didn't let the Doberman's lead slip. He took off, heading uphill and then heading left, picking up the road that led past the castle entrance and on up towards the Strahov Monastery. Behind him the shouts grew fainter. On he ran, the steep hill and cobbles making his lungs burn and his paws ache. And then, faintly, he heard from behind him the sound of the longer stride of the Doberman. Upwards the two dogs ran, but the race now was never in doubt. Hugo knew he could not outrun the Doberman, but he also knew, given a fair wind, he could outwit him. He stopped, turned around and, with his tail wagging and with his most amiable grin, waited for the Doberman to reach him. The guard dog skidded to a stop and looked perplexed.

'Soudruh, comrade, dobrý večer,' said Hugo – 'How nice of you to join me on my evening run. It gets terribly confined just being in the embassy garden.'

The Doberman looked even more perplexed. This wasn't going according to plan. There was supposed to be a run, a fight, a bit more of a fight, and then he would win. Instead, he was having a conversation with a civilised English Labrador who seemed to be a fluent Czech speaker. He needed guidance.

'Would you like to try a western dog chew? Had them flown in yesterday,' Hugo continued.

The Doberman, now miserably anxious because he didn't have a plan for this situation, nodded. Hugo woofed softly, twice, and two chews fell on the ground beneath his collar.

Hugo stepped back. 'Help yourself, be my guest.'

The Doberman, feeling that any action was better than being completely confused, helped himself.

'Dekuji!' – 'Thank you!' – he said, and moments later hit the cobbles, out cold.

Hugo sighed. That was the trouble with Dobermans. Had to follow the rules. No capacity for lateral thinking. The problem now was that the StB would be looking for him, and it would only be a matter of time before they found the unconscious guard dog and a full-scale hunt would be underway. He still had four hours to go before making the collection. He had to throw the secret police off the scent. His pursuers would expect him to either leave town, try and return to the embassy, or go to ground. He decided to convince them that he had left town.

He padded on, leaving Strahov behind him. After about ten minutes he stopped to listen. No sound of pursuit came, so, climbing a low wall beside the road, he settled down in the shadows to work out his next move. A passing LIAZ truck provided the opportunity he wanted and he jumped into the open back as it slowed for the corner, and then made himself inconspicuous amongst some building materials. He settled down to watch where the lorry was going. Initially it went west, but then turned down towards the river. Just before the river it stopped and Hugo heard voices. He swiftly realised they were at a police check point.

'Seen anyone on the road?'

'No, why?' came a voice from the cab.

'We're looking for an Englishman. His dog ran away and his owner has gone to ground. Keep your eyes open.'

Not much chance of that, thought Hugo, the lorry driver is bound to turn a blind eye to trouble unless he thinks someone's watching him.

'Perhaps he was Švejk,' laughed the lorry driver, 'out to do another dog sale. Why don't you try looking in Smichov?'

The policeman laughed. 'On your way,' he said, and the truck moved off over the river.

For a moment Hugo was diverted. What a country, where even the police and lorry drivers know that classic of Czech literature, The Good Soldier Švejk. Concentrate now, he thought, wondering which way the lorry would turn. He peered out into the darkness and sniffed deeply. The city lay downstream, to the left, but the lorry seemed to be going straight on. After a time, it turned and came to a halt by a builder's yard. Quickly looking around, Hugo jumped out whilst the driver was opening the yard gates, and melted once more into the shadows. The weather had changed and the rain had started now; a steady drizzle that would keep up for hours and, he hoped, wash away his scent from any tracking dogs. North of him, about a mile away, lay Vyšehrad, where he had planned to lie up before going to Old Town Square to make the exchange.

Moving quickly, taking care to avoid the pools of light cast by the occasional street lamp, he made his way north and up to the banks of the Vltava. Now for a bit of deception. He crossed the road and slid down the bank into the water. The cold hit him immediately as he drifted down between the island and the shore. Climbing out, he then crossed over a causeway for the next spit of land and headed towards some old rowing boats. He boarded one, chewed his way through the mooring line and waited for it to start to drift, before jumping back into the water again. That will give them something to think about when they find it empty on the next weir, he thought. Nothing like "foxing" the following pack.

There was only a little current here and he was able to swim to just below where the great mass of the Vyšehrad stood high over the river. Satisfied he had done all that he could to cover his tracks, he climbed out of the water again, shook himself dry and skirted round the base of the old fortress. Eventually he reached the trees by the side of Slavojova and, using their cover, he kept close to the fortress until he reached the top of Vratislavova. Thoroughly bedraggled, he then slipped through a part-open gate at the back of some houses and cautiously approached the back door. He barked quickly, quietly, once, and then again, and after what seemed an age he heard a key being turned and the door partly opened.

The smell of slow-cooked pork knuckle and red cabbage preceded the man that looked out. 'Dobrý večer,' he said.

'The wolves are hunting tonight,' said Hugo.

'Then we are best eating before a warm fire,' the man replied, and he opened the door to let Hugo in. 'Were you followed?' he asked as he closed the door behind him. 'The wolves really are hunting this time.'

Hugo recounted his story whilst the man led him further into the safe house.

'You'd best warm up and have a meal, but you can't stay here.'

'I know,' said Hugo. 'I still have things to do.' The man looked at him quizzically, but Hugo shook his head. 'Best not to know, but I will take a meal off you before I go.'

Hugo thought, what was it the old soldier used to say? "An army marches on its stomach . . ." How true, but I must keep that in perspective. Tonight is not a night for binge eating. Work to do. He thought of the other saying that was always on the old soldier's lips: "Duty, Hugo, duty. Duty to your comrades and duty to your Queen. Never forget." Hmm, thought Hugo, well someone betrayed us . . . because they were waiting for me. It must have been the cat.

The man helped him to portions of food from two large saucepans. Hugo waited whilst he served himself and started to eat.

'Just checking,' said Hugo. 'I know you'd expect me to bolt it down, but after tonight I can't trust anybody, not even you, my friend.'

The man laughed. 'Just like the old days' he said. 'Nothing changes. There is no trust in this business.'

Hugo finished his meal and got up to go. They went to the back door and looked out. The rain was coming down steadily now. Good, he thought, it will wash away any trace of me.

'Until the next time,' Hugo said.

The man looked at him. 'Go carefully, my loyal friend.'

'That's for certain,' said Hugo as he slipped into the night and was instantly lost to view.

For a while he stayed in the shadows, watching, but nobody moved and everything seemed normal. He moved on, down Vratislavova, past the hostelry named "At the Sign of the Golden Anchor" towards the bottom of the street. He crossed to the little wooded area, bare and empty in the winter, and waited until it was clear for him to slip across under the railway bridge. He then trotted down Vyšehradska, towards the centre of town. Quietly, he made his way to the Old Town Square and settled down in the shadows, once more to watch. The rain continued to fall, colder, mixed now with the odd snowflake. The Square was empty. The roasted chestnut sellers had packed up and gone home. Not much chance of anything, let alone a trdelnik, Nutella or normal now, thought Hugo as he quietly shook himself and silently gave thanks to the mediaeval builders who created arcades.

Satisfied that there was no-one on the lookout, he moved round towards the corner of Malé náměstí and Staroměstské náměstí. It wasn't time yet, but experience had taught him that if watchers were expecting something to happen at a certain time, they were more relaxed and careless the further in time they were away from the expected event. He settled further back into the shadows, confident that nobody could see him in the inky blackness. He waited. A door opened. Two men appeared, briefly silhouetted by the light inside, which was promptly turned off. Hugo shrank further back, conscious that his heart was beginning to beat a little faster. Then two more took up position across from the corner of Malé náměstí. This is a trap, thought Hugo, best wait, they don't know I'm here but they are expecting something.

He smelt the man before he heard him, as very faintly, born downwind, came the characteristic smell of communist cigarettes, cheap aftershave and lack of a recent bath. Hugo stiffened. All his senses were alert. One man or two? Was that a dog he could hear? He relaxed. One man, crossing Malé náměstí. He could see him now. He could sense the man's uneasiness. But if this was his contact, it was too dangerous to move.

Suddenly the man reached into his pocket and pulled out something: a faint movement had given away one of the watchers. Hugo heard the muffled "plop" of a silenced shot, and one of the watchers fell to the ground. A fusillade of shots then rang out, and the man he was watching crumpled. As the watchers came to inspect their kill, Hugo quietly slipped away. Time to go, treachery was afoot.

Getting out of the city was easy. He headed south until he got to Komořany, cautiously crossed the two bridges at Lahovice and then headed west. The rain came down relentlessly, and he was glad for the extra layer of fat he had built up. By daybreak he had covered nearly thirty miles, and he settled up in a forest about ten miles east of Rakovnik.

Now the real battle began. With hunger. The weak part of his plan had always been food. To stay concealed he needed to stay away from people; to eat he had to find food near them. Dogs were not popular in communist Czechoslovakia, because you had to have an expensive licence. What dogs there were in the countryside were generally not friendly. And any dogs he encountered would be likely to make a lot of noise.

Hugo, old boy, he thought to himself, you've done it now. No more fantasising about the strong silent heroic Labrador, this is for real. And, with that deeply unpleasant thought, he curled up under a tree root and with an insistently rumbling tummy tried to get some rest.

The weather slowly improved as the day wore on, but the thoughts of food became more pronounced. He turned his mind to wolves, remembering that whilst they needed about a kilogram of meat a day they could survive for weeks, if needed, without any food at all. Weeks, thought Hugo with a shudder, it's been over eighteen hours since that pork knuckle and I am starving already. Then he thought, it's no use thinking like this. I have a hundred miles still to go and staying here thinking about food isn't going to help. Dusk was drawing in now, it was time to move.

Reaching the edge of a wood, he looked out over fields. Some deer were on the woodland edge and they moved back into cover when they saw him. Not much chance of me bothering you, thought Hugo as he moved cautiously around the field edge.

He settled down to a purposeful walk. A comfortable four miles an hour should bring him near to Bochov before he had to find somewhere to lie up for the day. He mulled over the events of the previous day. Somebody, or some animal, had clearly betrayed the plan. My money is on the cat, he thought. They will want me dead now, as I am the only one who can confirm the treachery. Again, insistently, thoughts of food crept into his head, and however hard he tried to banish them they reappeared. Images of dropped containers of chicken biryani floated before his eyes, and long-forgotten smells of the biscuit factory next to where he grew up surfaced in his mind. Just one trip into a passing village, he thought. There's bound to be a bin to empty, or some food to blag. And then the admonition came back: "Duty, Hugo, duty." He thought of his time in Cornwall, and how they had taught him mindfulness, and then he thought of Zoe. A wave of desolation surged over him as he recollected how his food addiction had cost him the one great love of his life. He stifled a howl and trotted on. Mustn't ruminate. Think of the positives. You're doing something useful for once.

The intrusive thoughts settled and he took note of his surroundings. The moon was up now, and clouds scudded across the sky as the earlier breeze strengthened and shifted into the north-east. He didn't like this. This meant more cold, and the possibility of snow. He quickened his pace. If it was to snow then he really would need food. The going would get more difficult, and he would have to take more care over leaving tracks. If he could get to the forest just south of Bochov, he could then make his way through the forest during the day, and sneak in to Karlovy Vary the next night in search of food.

Thoughts of Zoe wouldn't leave his head. The nights of saying her name as he half slept, with his face to the wall. The anguish of her not being there, the memory of the touch of her paws during the night, of the relaxation that comes for all animals when they know they can share the watch because they can trust their pack. He remembered his friend Marmalade, who used to curl up with him sometimes after Zoe was lost; how Marmalade always seemed to sense when he was sleepy and take over the watch, allowing him the occasional deep sleep that banished the bad dreams. Then there would be the paw swipe across the nose, and "Wake up, you lazy Labrador, my turn for a kip!" And he would watch whilst Marmalade curled herself into a ball beside him and put a paw over her eyes to shut out the street lights. What a cat! But even Marmalade was lost to him now. They'd been partners in addiction, but he hadn't seen Marmalade since he'd found this chance of redemption by working for the K9 section of MI6. They always did recruit the streetwise dropouts. The thought jolted him. Must concentrate. Keep going.

The first snowflakes came on the wind. A light flurry and then nothing. Hugo experienced a moment of panic. He still felt the insistent hunger that always started within ten minutes of a meal, but now he was feeling something different; he was starting to experience a feeling of cold and weakness that he knew could not be ignored. So long as he could keep his pace up he could maintain his body temperature, but if he were to slow and stop he knew would risk the spiral of cold and sleep that would end in failure and death. Food was becoming a priority. He dug deeper and quickened his pace again.

Baking is hot and absorbing work. The baker of Bochov had started at three the previous afternoon, mixing, putting dough aside to rise, knocking back and then allowing it to rise again. The heat of his ovens was stifling, and despite the winter cold the top half of the bakery stable door was open to provide some relief. Hugo sat in the shadows outside, almost driven mad by the smell of freshly baked bread. What was it they said back in Cornwall? "Work on delayed gratification; everything comes to he who waits."

He waited. From inside the bakery he could hear a radio playing over the sound of the machinery. Soon, from the house beside, he heard a call, 'Snídaně, breakfast!' Breakfast? he thought. It's five in the morning. That I should be so lucky to find breakfast that early. The call came again, louder now, and the radio was turned down. "What?" bellowed a voice from within the bakery. 'Breakfast!' came the voice again, this time with a tinge of exasperation. Hugo shrank further back into the shadows as the stable door was fully opened and a large, flustered man, covered in flour, came out and went into the house. The bakery door was left open. Seizing his moment, Hugo stepped inside and looked around. Loaves of bread were cooling on wire racks just inside the door; a tray of rye loaves, ready to be baked, stood on a table; and in the corner, was a large oven from which emerged the smell that had drawn him there. Very carefully Hugo took a loaf from the bottom of the cooling rack and quickly returned to the shadows. None too soon. He had expected the baker to eat his breakfast in the house, but he had simply collected it and come back to work. He banged the bottom half of the door shut, turned up the radio, and set to his trade once more. Hugo listened. The radio announcer was talking about the shooting in Malé náměstí, and how the authorities were looking for a British spy and his dog. Bother, he thought. He had hoped to snaffle two loaves, but one would have to do and, setting aside the eating habits of a lifetime, he resisted the temptation to eat it on the spot and retreated to the woods a couple of hundred yards away.

It was just past five in the morning now. He had another three hours of dark and dawn before he reached the forest, but the bread had given him new energy and hope. He had made much better progress than he could have hoped. All he had to do was reach the forest the other side of Bochov and he could then lay up for a while, knowing he could circle south of Karlovy Vary, under cover, and in daylight, if needed. He started off again.

A song ran through his head, "My old man said follow the van, and don't dilly-dally on the way . . ." Not much chance of dilly-dallying with the StB looking out for me, he thought, but the song persisted in his head. He shivered and increased his pace. The snow was falling again, coming down in big wet flakes that gradually accumulated on the ground. On he went. He thought of Zoe again and his mood turned to misery. He remembered how he had messed up his life because of his constant craving for food and how, in turn, he had messed up the lives of his friends. Sad, the way the problems of one person ripple out to affect the lives of so many others. I'm a bad apple, he thought to himself – old phrases in language always have meaning. He couldn't change any of what he had done; he couldn't really, in any meaningful way, make amends; but perhaps he could seek redemption by doing his duty. He was slowing now, getting cold.

The forest, when he reached it, was silent. No predawn activity as the animals made final forays before merging into the background and disappearing for the day. Just a tomb-like silence. Not even the trees were talking, as the wind had dropped and the snow fell, gently, steadily, vertically, sliding off the branches onto the ground. Hugo shivered again. I must find shelter.

Shelter came in the shape of a leaf-filled hollow under the roots of a tree that had been blown over in a storm. He burrowed into the leaves, twirled and settled down. The hunger was insistent again; real hunger, not the hunger of his addiction but the hunger of a body that desperately needed fuel to carry on. More insistent was sleep. He had travelled far and his body craved rest.

Hours later he woke. The forest was still silent, apart from the occasional caw from a crow. He padded on, making slightly north of west, giving an airfield a wide berth, to where the fringes of the forest met the southern outskirts of Karlovy Vary.

He sat in the shadows on the edge of the trees and looked across at the back of a grand hotel. A single outside light illuminated the back door to the kitchen. He waited. Funny, he mused, doesn't matter whether it's a capitalist or a communist country, the big guys always look after themselves. From the hotel, the smell of cooking drifted across to him. He waited patiently, despite the rising pangs of hunger. Food wasn't sending him crazy now. He knew what would happen and he could wait. Sure enough, after a while, the door opened and a kitchen porter appeared with a bucket, which he emptied into a bin outside. The porter looked around at the banks of snow and lit a cigarette. Even though it was cold outside it was hot work in a kitchen, and cooling off was always welcome. Eventually, he finished his cigarette, threw the butt into the snow, shivered and shut the door behind him. Hugo waited, to make sure that the coast was clear, and then moved under cover to the closest point to the bins. Quietly he stole across the little bit of open ground to the back of the hotel, checked the bin and then pushed it forward gently into a small snow bank. The lid rolled off, its noise muffled by the snow. Hugo helped himself to the contents, his first full meal since liberating the loaf in Bochov. He made short work of the leftovers and then, just as quietly, withdrew into the darkness of the forest as the snow covered his tracks once more.

Deep into the forest he went, still heading west. He walked for about an hour, stumbling through the undergrowth in the darkness. Eventually, more by smell and touch, he found another fallen tree to shelter under. He twirled around in the leaf litter once more, and went to sleep. The snow began again in earnest.

Sometime later he woke. Start of day five. Half his allotted time gone. It was just beginning to get light; the cold hard light where the grey light of the sky is reflected back by the white blanket that covered the ground. It was still snowing. Inside the forest, Hugo was protected from the worst of this, but every low branch that he brushed against deposited snow over him – but it obliterated his tracks.

Now, he thought, the final push. He struck out again, through the forest. Southwest at first, keeping the River Ohre on his right. The tree cover thinned here, and there was more habitation. The snow made the going difficult, but the gloom aided him, and people were more concerned about going about their own business than taking note of an occasional black shadow silhouetted against the snow that then merged once more into the forest edge.

He changed direction further south as he approached Sokolov, to avoid the huge lignite mining complex. Could do without this, he thought, as he detoured around it for several hours. Night was upon him again. The detour had taken longer than he hoped and he would have to rest up. Time was running out.

Again, he found shelter in the forest. With rest came space for thoughts of crossing the border. It would have to be at nightfall, and where it ran through the trees. Find cover until the last few minutes and find time to observe the Pohraničí Straz, the specialist border guard, before making his move. Then, flooding in again, came the feelings of remorse over his addiction. In the past he had gone through the motions with his apologies, but he had to admit they had not really been genuine, and he had used his character to charm people. He recognised the role that fear was playing in his, apparent, true remorse. See how it is if you get out of this, Hugo me boy, he said to himself. He settled to a watchful rest.

The cold was in his bones now, and the urge to sleep was almost insurmountable. Food had been forgotten a long time ago as the enormous weariness that presaged a longed-for deep sleep threatened to engulf him. If I sleep I will die, he thought, I must stay awake, I must.

In the predawn he started again. He was now in the border area. He needed to be more cautious as only carefully screened party members were allowed to live here, and anything unusual would be likely to arouse suspicion. Again, wherever he could, he kept just inside of the forest edge and stuck to hedgerows and ditch margins where he had to cross fields. He was getting closer now. He had arranged his own crossing spot before he went to Prague. It was the weakest part of his plan, because he relied on others to make it work – a dangerous ploy in his world of shifting loyalties. Someone had knowledge of their plans, or why else would the StB have been on the lookout in Prague?

By daybreak he was in his final stretch of forest. He crept quietly through the undergrowth until he could observe the border. It stretched away in front of him. The road the patrol was on. The watchtowers in sight of each other, and the fence made of multiple strands of close-spaced, rusting barbed wire. Somewhere in that fence, where the bottom strands of wire were covered by snow and vegetation, should be a break just big enough for him to squeeze through. The wind had shifted to the west and borne on it came the faint smell of WD40. Hugo relaxed a little. Just as he had asked. Nothing visual to identify the break – which at someone's great peril had been cut two nights before – just a characteristic smell to guide him in. Now to watch the watchers.

Occasional murmurs of conversation came from the tower nearest him – banter between two bored sentries. They were talking about watching for a dog. 'Not a chance of seeing one,' he heard, 'Švejk would have found it and sold it as a dachshund to some unsuspecting idiot.' He heard laughter, and noticed the smell of cigarette smoke mixed with the sulphurous smell of a just-struck match. He had asked for the break to be cut as close as possible to this watchtower. Experience had taught him that watchers always had the mindset that a crossing attempt would be made as far away from a watchtower as possible, therefore his only risk would be when the guards came down when they changed shift. He waited patiently.

Again, with inactivity came the cold. He knew he had only one chance. He was worried about failing but, in some ways, he was even more worried about succeeding. He had confronted his demons on this trip and, to a large extent, conquered them. If he got through, though, he would have to live a different life. There would be the inevitable debrief. Had he given the game away? What was the evidence for implicating the embassy cat? He would probably not be trusted again. He would have to find another job. He shivered. He waited. The day wore on and dusk came. Just before dusk the guards changed, and he waited for the new guards to settle. The cold would get to them soon enough, and then they would open their Thermos bottles.

Eventually, he heard the sound of feet stamping and blowing on hands to warm them up. Distracted, thought Hugo. Slowly and quietly he moved out of the forest edge.

He sniffed carefully. The strongest smell came from slightly to the right, closer to the watchtower. He flattened himself to the snow so that there was no distinct silhouette, just a black blob against the white. He was at the fence now. The smell of WD40 was strong and, in the gloom, he could dimly make out the cut ends of the lower three strands. Slowly he inched his way forward. The wire gave way before him. His heart pounding, he continued to inch his way forward. Head, and then shoulders. He gave a little mental thanks that after the last few days' diet his shoulders were back to being the broadest part of him. Hips now, and he was through.

He knew he still had another hundred metres to go before the actual border line, but he was past all the obstructions.

Fifty metres to go.

Twenty-five.

He was just beginning to relax, when there was a sudden brilliant light and something hit him in the side.

So close, thought Hugo, as he tried, vainly, to run.

Chapter 13

New Beginnings

The vet put in his normal morning telephone call to us.

'I think it's safe to wake him up now,' he said. 'His pulse rate has come right down and he seems to be doing a lot of dreaming, judging by the way his paws are twitching. He's also started to fart a lot, I'm afraid, but it's a good sign. Means his gut is beginning to work properly.'

We went down to see him. Hugo had been left in a darkened area and was sound asleep when we arrived. His paws were twitching and the odd woof and growl drifted up from his bed.

The vet switched the lights on. Hugo woke with a start, looking very disoriented.

'Uncle Herriot,' he said, looking at the vet with a very puzzled expression. Turning his head, he caught sight of us. 'Hello, Yer Ladyship,' he added, looking at his mistress. 'Guv, what are you all doing here?' He tried to get up but his paws gave way. 'I must have been dreaming, give me a moment or two, there's something I need to remember.' And he promptly fell asleep again.

'You can take him home now,' said the vet. 'He'll be a bit

groggy for a few days but he should be fine after that. It will take a while for him to get his strength back, though.'

I carried Hugo back to the car.

'Not too heavy for you am I, guv?'

'No, Hugo, your little escapade has got you back below thirty kilos, where you are supposed to be.'

'Had ever such an exciting dream.'

'Oh yes, you found yourself in the Harrods food hall all on your own?'

I got the withering look that he always reserved for what he regarded as my grosser pieces of sarcasm.

'I will not deign to reply to that, guv,' he said. 'Suffice it to say that I think I may, finally, have conquered my food addiction.'

'Well, Hugo, you've had about a week of an enforced diet, does that count?'

'I'll have you know that I am a reformed Labrador. I shall even give up my membership of the Amalgamated Society of Biscuit Muggers and Food Snafflers.'

'Steady on, old lad, we would be delighted if you did, but you are still getting over the effects of your anaesthetic.'

Hugo grunted and settled back in his bed again. 'You wait,' he said, and went to sleep once more.

***

Later that day he achieved a first. He remained on his bed whilst his mistress prepared his food, and didn't move until he was told that his supper was ready. Later still, he watched me prepare our supper, passing the odd helpful comment: 'Not enough pesto with that beetroot salad,' and

'I think a steak that thick will need two and a half hours in the sous vide,' without stirring from his repose in the corner of the kitchen.

A bit later we heard, 'Would you mind taking down me collection of food wrappers and painting the wall?'

'You're serious about this, aren't you?'

'Never been more so. I've turned over a new leaf.' And with that Hugo told us what he could remember about his dream.

'So, you really were taking notice when your mistress and I sat talking about the past over supper?'

''I'm a very observant Labrador, guv, besides which, 'Er Ladyship had an exciting time in Eastern Europe. I thought you could include some of this for colour when you get round to writing your book.'

'Thank you, Hugo. Anyway, how are you feeling? Ready to try a little walk?'

'Just a little one, guv, still feeling a bit wobbly.'

We took a stroll into Bigwood. It had rained and fresh, earthy smells enticed Hugo off the path. He had always been a great one for digging around tree roots.

'I used to be a truffle hound in a previous existence,' he said.

'Didn't know you believed in reincarnation, Hugo?'

'Course I do. Only way to make sense of the world,' came the reply.

But this time, after a cursory sniff, he moved on. After a couple of hundred yards he reappeared at my heel.

'Can we go home?'

'Feeling tired?'

'Knackered.'

'Come on, then. Bedtime.'

We slowly walked home.

'Don't you feel the need for something to get your strength up?'

'Stop tempting me, guv, it won't work. I'm a reformed Labrador.'

***

The next morning Hugo was up early.

'Go back to bed, Hugo.'

'But, guv–'

'Bed.'

A sigh followed, and a couple of twirls around his bed, another big sigh, and then a long, persistent, and entirely fake snore.

'OK, Hugo, what's on your mind?'

'Feeling better, guv. It's a hot day so I thought an early morning walk was called for. Besides which, I've got stuff to do.'

'OK, I'm getting up.'

I made coffee. Hugo did his usual security patrol, inspecting the perimeter of the garden whilst he waited for me. He referred to it as "checking for leaks", although why he affected this piece of naval slang I had no idea. He had a long-standing battle with the local foxes, who would wait until the house was locked up for the night and then peer in through the sitting room window just to wind him up. Having satisfied himself that there were no new breaches in his defences, he came back in muttering, 'I still don't know how they get in. I'll catch them at it one day.'

I gave Hugo his morning pills. This was a ritual known in the house as "pill parade". He had the common Labrador problem of arthritis in his hips, not aided by years of being overweight and sleeping rough. Although his medication helped 'wiv [his] arferitis', he had a particular aversion to one capsule that, as always, had to be inserted into a piece of soft cheese. I was never sure whether it was a real aversion, or just another of his ploys to get a favourite foodstuff, but a triangle of Laughing Cow cream cheese was dutifully unwrapped and filled with his painkiller. (Any deviation from this resulted in the offending capsule being spat out, and a despairing look on his face that said, can't I trust you to get anything right?)

By half past six we were on the Heath.

'What have you got to do that's so important?' I asked.

'Need to have a discussion about me therapist's licence with "the powers that be". They've been a bit touchy about me for a while, and me recent fall from grace won't have helped at all.'

'I see. I think they're likely to want solid evidence that you really have changed before they start to trust you again.'

'I know. It's always the dilemma. There are so many times an addict says, "I've really changed," when they know, inside, that they're lying. And then there is the time, like now, when you know you really have changed and you know nobody is going to believe you.'

'Problem of "crying wolf"'.

'Exactly.'

'I thought that was a forbidden word?'

'Told you, it's all different now.'

We walked on. Hugo ambled over to a group of dogs that were playing whilst their owners chatted. I found a bench and sat down to enjoy the early morning sun.

Hugo's mistress and I had a problem. Uncle Herriot had advised that we did not tell Hugo about Zoe until he was well on his way to recovery. The time had obviously come, but how would he take it? He seemed to be deliberately avoiding the subject and we would, clearly, have to bring it up with him.

I called my friend.

'I know we talked about it the other day, but I have been thinking about telling Hugo about Zoe.'

'Glad you mentioned it, I was just thinking the same.'

'Time for a family conference.'

'Tonight?'

"I think so.'

'Done.'

We chatted for a bit and then rang off.

Hugo came back.

'Can we go back now, guv. I've got a confession to make, and it'll be a bit easier after I've had me breakfast.'

We walked back in silence. Hugo looked thoroughly dejected and I wondered what was on his mind. He sat on his downstairs bed, surveying the blank spaces on the wall where his food wrappers had been whilst I prepared his food.

'Ta, Guv,' he said as I put his bowl down.

I made a coffee and waited for him to finish.

'What's on your mind?' I asked.

'Don't really know how to tell you. 'Er Ladyship will be very upset with me.'

'Don't try and wrap it up, Hugo, just spit it out. Saves all the trouble of worrying about the words.'

'I'm . . . not really a therapist, guv, I didn't finish me course.'

'I'm not surprised.'

'You guessed?'

‘‘Well, you did seem to have a remarkable lack of clients, and you clearly weren't in control of your addiction.'

‘'Er Ladyship will be really cross with me.'

‘I think you'll find she'll be very understanding.'

Hugo sat looking woeful.

‘Zoe kept on at me about starting on me studies. That was before I ended up in the dogs home and went into rehab. “I'm so proud of you, Hugo,” she would say to encourage me, but I knew deep down me laziness and me addiction kept me from studying. I could tell you all the good words, but actually getting on with it, that were something different. Anyway, after a bit I stopped studying, and used to spend me days out on the streets in a different part of London so Zoe wouldn't find out. Then one day she did. We had a frightful row, I raided a chocolate cake, and when I come out of hospital she'd gone. The rest you know.'

‘Poor old Hugo. It's a common story with addicts. Without being unkind they always lie and deceive, and it's always their loved ones who are caught in this tangled mess of love and despair.'

‘I know, guv. Anyway, now that I have finally seen the light, thought I should tell you.'

‘You'll have to tell 'Er Ladyship yourself, you know.'

‘I know, I'm dreading doing that.'

He sat on his bed looking really pathetic. He was completely deflated.

‘What am I going to do, guv? I've made such a mess of things. I really wanted to be a therapist dog. They started me on a therapy course at the end of rehab; they really believed I could turn over a new leaf. I looked up to them down there in Cornwall, but never thought I could make the grade.'

'Hugo, you've been the one telling me to believe in myself. You know yourself that "the past is the past" however hard it is to really grasp the concept. We can't alter the past, but we can be kind to ourselves and recognise that we did the best we could at the time. I'm sure that was true for you, but you just hadn't reached the turning point in your addiction to food. Now you can say, "I've turned the corner," and you can work to make things better in the future. I have to say I think you would make a great therapist.'

'Kind of you to say so, but that's not how it feels. I've messed everything up. It would be nice to see Zoe again. I doubt she'd want to see me, though. Did your brother find her?'

I decided to seize the opportunity. 'We've been so worried about you that we decided not to tell you until you were better. But, yes, Zoe has been found.'

Hugo stood up, trembling.

'I can't meet her, guv. She'll not want to have anything to do with me. Not after I've messed up so much.'

'Hugo.'

'Yes, guv?'

'I think she would love to see you. You could always go back to your course and show how much you've reformed. Why don't we get in touch with the therapy school?'

'Not worth it.'

'Why not?'

'They wouldn't have me back.'

'Have you tried?'

'Not worth it.'

He laid down again and curled up into an even tighter ball in the corner of his bed.

I left him. Experience had taught me that when he was like this sleep was the best medicine. Besides which, I needed to talk to his mistress about how he was.

I called her.

'Can't say much because he might overhear the conversation, but Hugo's very low again today. I told him about Zoe. I've never known him so negative, and yet he's done so well.'

'I'll be home soon. Let's take him for a walk in Kenwood. He always likes that.'

Hugo was not amused at being roused from his slumbers to go on another walk. He was even less amused at being told it was for his own good. He refused to jump into the back of the car.

'It's too high, I can't manage it anymore,' he grumbled. We got the ramp and helped him up. 'Haven't got the energy. You'll have me using a doggy Zimmer frame next.'

With Hugo still protesting, we drove off. When we got to the car park he looked around and sniffed.

'Very nice,' he said. 'Can we go home now?'

'No,' we replied very firmly.

He looked at us in puzzlement. 'Keep yer hair on. It's bad enough one of us feeling mardy.'

He hopped out of the car and sat down.

'What's this?' I asked.

'Waiting for me lead to be put on.'

'What?'

'Haven't you seen the sign? "All Dogs Must Be Kept On A Lead"?'

He looked so serious and forlorn that we had to stifle the giggles.

'Alright, Hugo, but it's only for a hundred yards you know.'

'Them's the rules.'

He trotted along beside us until we took his lead off at the entrance to the park, when he veered off into the long grass in search of interesting sniffs.

'He's been really down today. Started pretty normal, but went downhill during his morning walk. He seems full of remorse and negativity. I've tried to encourage him. He told me he dropped out of therapy school. He mentioned Zoe as well, which was why I told him she'd been found. I think it must be a reaction to the traumas of the chocolate cake and then being sedated for so long.'

His mistress nodded. 'He was in a very bad way when I originally got him from the Labrador rescue place. He'd been kept in a cage when his previous owners went out. They then overfed him to compensate for their guilt at leaving him like that. Poor old lad. With his history before they got him it couldn't have been worse. They caged him, of course, to stop him going back on the streets. He was nearly twice his proper weight when he arrived with me. It was such a struggle getting his weight down, he used to look at food so pathetically.'

We walked on. Hugo rootled around in a distracted sort of way, occasionally coming back for a bit of contact, but then going off again. He seemed lost in a world of his own.

Eventually he came back and said, 'Guv, can we find a bench to sit down? I've got something to tell me mistress.'

We found a convenient bench. Hugo wandered around in an agitated way and then came over.

'Yes, Hugo?' she asked.

'I'm a fraud.'

'Of course you are.'

Hugo looked astonished. 'Has the guv told you?'

'No, he told me that you had a confession to make, that he knew what it was, but that you needed to tell me yourself.'

'I'm not really a therapist dog. I dropped out before I finished. It was me addiction. I'm so sorry.'

Hugo looked utterly woebegone.

His mistress, however, was quite no-nonsense. 'Well, Hugo,' she said, 'I know you're a food addict, and I know addicts tell stories and can't be trusted. Just think of all the times we've had to set guard on the food when we're laying a table, and it's even worse with a barbecue.'

Hugo looked even more woebegone. 'It's not going to be another rehoming, is it?' he said.

'Whatever gave you that idea? We love you, and always will. We are not going to give up on you just when you've turned a corner. Of course not. Never forget that you're part of the family. And we have found Zoe. Life could be wonderful for you. But you have to prove yourself now. We will all support you.'

'How can I prove myself?'

'By going back and finishing your course.'

'But they won't have me.'

'How do you know?

Hugo sighed.

'You're assuming. You haven't checked, have you?' we both said at once.

'Look,' said his mistress. 'I know you've had a really hard day and you feel thoroughly defeated, but let's not have any more stories. I'll help you get in touch with the therapy school tomorrow and see if we can get you back in.'

'Thanks, Yer Ladyship,' said an even more unhappy Hugo. 'Can we go home now?'

'Of course.'

'Please don't do anymore about Zoe, for the moment. I couldn't bear seeing her again having let her down so badly.'

'Not for the moment, Hugo. But that is another relationship you have to put right.'

'Bet she's found someone else.'

'That's a bridge you may have to cross.'

***

Later that evening we rang the dogs home where Hugo had spent so much time after the Great Jermyn Street Cheese Heist. They remembered Hugo very well, and gave us the address and phone number of the retreat he had been sent to in Cornwall.

The next morning, we rang them and spoke to the head of the therapy school and explained what had happened. It seemed Hugo had been quite a model pupil, and had done so well in his rehabilitation that he had been fast-tracked into therapy training. It had all gone wrong when he was sent back up to London to finish one of his modules. He had been delivered to the door of his temporary digs, but the driver of the van he had come up in had then driven off without handing him over to his landlady. It seemed Hugo had just wandered off, and then disappeared, and nobody had heard anything more about him. The lady at the other end of the phone was really pleased to know that he was alright. He had been quite a favourite. We asked if they would have him back to continue his course.

'Of course. He'll have to come back down here for an assessment, and we'll have to find out how much he remembers so we can work out where to start him, but we would love to see him again. We've got a new course starting at the end of next week. Perhaps you could bring him down then?'

And with that, Hugo's future for the next few months was decided.

After the phone call we told Hugo what had been arranged.

'Do I get a say in this?' he said, slightly grumpily. 'Seems like everybody is making my decisions for me.'

'Sorry, Hugo, we thought that was what you wanted. You don't have to go.'

'Of course I do. Just having you on. I think you two are a pair of diamonds. I'm ever so excited. But promise me one thing . . .'

'What's that?'

'If Zoe still wants to see me you won't tell her I've gone back to finish me course. I'd like to do that myself.'

'We promise.'

***

The following weekend we loaded Hugo and his memory foam bed into the back of the car and drove him down. Hugo kept up a running commentary about his first drive down and all his queries about names.

'Still puzzled by this name Cornwall. A food origin seems so much more likely to me. I really fancy the idea of Shredded Wheatshire.'

'Actually, Hugo, not much wheat or corn is grown in Cornwall, and it really wasn't named after food.'

'Why did you wander off when you came up to London on the course, Hugo?' his mistress then asked.

'Dunno really,' he replied. 'I think it had a lot to do with being back in London, with all the triggers about me previous life. Although a lot of bad stuff happened, there was a lot of fun as well. I thought to meself, I'll just go and look up Bonzo and Marmalade and have a chin wag, and one thing led to another and I was back on the streets again–'

'You didn't tell me about this episode, Hugo?' I interjected.

'Never got round to it, guv. Thing is, that it had been ever such a long time since I'd last seen me mates. There was all that time in the dogs home and then in the retreat in Cornwall. I thought I could handle it. Bonzo and me had got on so well, and he and I and Marmalade had made such a fantastic team. She were a good lookout for Bonzo and me. Poor little lass, she really fancied being a getaway driver. Can you imagine, a little ginger cat that can't see over the top of the steering wheel, high on catnip, and at the controls of a powerful car? "Marmalade," we used to say, "you've been watching too many episodes of The Sweeney, stick to climbing trees and telling us what's going on."

'Anyway, after a while I got caught and taken to a dog pound. And after that they sent me to another rehoming centre, and I got taken on by some folk who fed me well enough, but kept me in a cage when they went out for the day. After a bit they couldn't cope, so it was back to being rehomed and I ended up with 'Er Ladyship. She done me a power of good. The rest you know.'

'So how do you know it will be different now?'

'I just do. Something really has changed inside. I can't explain it. I think it's got a lot to do with being older and wiser, and being looked after and understood. Me walks with you helped a lot. There was a lot to get off me chest.'

'I thought you said that was your therapy model?'

'Yes, but you were very understanding and knew stuff, even though I kept shutting you up. It was actually very comforting and helpful.'

'You really are a rogue.'

'Humph,' said Hugo, and went to sleep for the last twenty miles to his destination.

Chapter 14

The Old Abbey School for Therapy Dogs

We turned off down a narrow road that followed the twists and turns of an estuary. We were surrounded by ancient woodland that permitted only the occasional glimpse of the sea, and nothing at all of our destination until we burst out of the trees into parkland and saw the house in front of us. The house was huge – we were later to learn that it had half an acre of leaky roof. In appearance it looked more like a terrace of grand houses behind which loomed the bulk of a rather splendid parish church. Hugo directed us round the back to a gravelled area, where we parked the car and got out.

He led us across to a freshly painted door with a polished brass plaque beside it. We went in and found a large, comfortable-looking lady seated behind a desk on which stood a sign, "The Old Abbey School for Therapy Dogs".

'We seem to have come to the right place?' I said.

'Don't mind him,' chimed in Hugo. 'He was always good at the bleeding obvious.'

The lady smiled. 'Good to see you back, Hugo, glad you haven't lost your sense of humour.'

Hugo grunted. 'Afternoon, Kerensa,' he said. 'Just checking in. Been a bit of an idiot, and coming back to finish me course.'

'That's fine, my lover,' said the lady, 'just come with me, all of you, and I'll show you Hugo's quarters. Then we can have a cup of tea. I'm sure you're parched after such a long journey.'

We went back outside, across a courtyard and through an old oak door set into a Gothic arch. A circle of dog kennels stretched away, each with a tiled floor and a little covered shelter at each end, one enclosed for sleeping during the night, the other open so that a dog could lie there and watch the world go by. The kennels were arranged in such a way that the day-end of the kennel was at the centre of the circle, so that the dogs could all chat with each other.

Hugo looked around.

'Cor,' he said, 'this brings back some memories. See how it's arranged. It's brilliant. You can always retreat back into your night-time kennel for a bit of privacy, or you can lay out in the centre, have a daydream, chat to your mates, or even engage in a bit of group therapy.'

Kerensa opened the gate to one of the quarters.

'Come along now, Hugo,' she said, 'you can leave your bag in your kennel.'

We put Hugo's overnight bag down. It contained the usual stuff: collapsible dog bowl for when travelling, a comb and brush, two towels, and his favourite toys – two much-loved cuddly zebras and a squeaky banana that was just small enough for him to pick up and bring as a greeting to friends and family.

Having had a quick look around and admired his surroundings, we went with Kerensa in search of the cup of tea.

'Now, don't worry about Hugo, he'll be well cared for,' she said. 'He can Facetime home every evening – after the first couple of weeks – to let you know how he's getting on. We have that little gap to let him settle down properly. He will have to be assessed to see how much he remembers of the course he did and whether he really has turned a corner.'

A discreet cough came from Hugo. 'Excuse me. Talk over me head, why don't you? I can understand, and I do have feelings.' He looked at us mournfully. 'Nobody really trusts me, do they?'

'Hugo,' said Kerensa, 'you of all people should know the score with addicts. They always have their illness. It's just a question of whether they are truly in recovery or not.'

Hugo looked even more doleful. 'Well, I certainly am, but a little bit of trust would help me on my way.'

We were saved from a difficult moment by the arrival of tea. Hugo perked up when he saw the tea tray, but confined himself to just one cucumber sandwich and a bowl of water.

He came out to say goodbye afterwards.

I'll be alright, Yer Ladyship, guv. It's a great honour to be given a second chance. I really will try to make this work. Can't say any more than that.'

'Good luck, Hugo,' we said, and watched him walk back towards his kennels.

'Time to go, Your Ladyship, parting is always difficult,' he called over his shoulder.

We left and found a hotel for the night and drove back to London the next day.

***

The house seemed very empty without Hugo around. I suddenly realised how much a part of the furniture he was. The day had always started with, 'Where's me breakfast, guv?' To which the reply was always, 'After your morning walk.' There would then be the ritual grumbling from Hugo: 'I really don't need to work up an appetite and make sure we are back in time for "Thought for the Day!"' I had introduced Hugo to this. I always used to listen to it when I got into work, before I saw my patients. Hugo loved it, and if he heard a thought he particularly liked he would repeat the story a few times and then try and use it as an example when he was trying to be a therapist with me.

After his walk and breakfast, he would then sleep in his day-bed in the kitchen, apparently dead to the world until the fridge or the larder was opened, when he would suddenly appear by one's side. 'What's it to be today, guv?' he would then ask. 'I can see the makings of a very good fish soup there. Make sure you leave out the mussels and put in plenty of tomato and saffron.'

These interjections formed the backdrop of the day, and being without them made his absence even harder. He had promised he would Facetime us every evening as soon as he was allowed, and as the days went past we became more and more keen to talk to him. He had, of course, already instructed his mistress to set up his own ringtone and, right on time, two weeks' later, the strains of "I'm an Urban Spaceman" by, of course, The Bonzo Dog Doo-Dah Band rang out.

'Yer Ladyship, guv, I'm having a lovely time.'

'How are things going, Hugo?'

'Quite hard work. They set me a test to see what I could remember and it seems I did alright. It's a bit lonely, though.

Got used to having you two around and looking out for me. Haven't been able to get to know me classmates properly yet. I don't do very well in new environments, I find them a bit scary.'

'But you've been there before?'

'I know. The layout and everything is the same. And Kerensa is still there doing the admin. But a lot of the staff have changed. It's lonely at night, even though it's easy to have a chat.'

'You can always call us now. We miss you, Hugo, the house isn't the same without you. Do you get the radio in the morning?'

'Fortunately, and I do get a good bit of meditation time. Trying hard not to meditate on chicken biryani.' He chuckled. 'Just having you on. I'll be alright. It's a lot better than being on the streets. Got to go now, but you've got to push the red button, my paw can't manage it.'

'When are you going to call next?'

'At the weekend. I'll send a postcard tomorrow.'

'Take care, Hugo'

'Night-night.'

I touched the button on the screen and he faded from view. I looked at his mistress, and I could see she was thinking the same as me.

'I hope this is going to work,' she said.

'It's early days yet.'

'I hope you're right.'

***

The next few days passed slowly. My friend went away on business and I settled back into writing and the occasional trip down to the Imperial War Museum to research the background to my book. Sure enough, Hugo's postcard dropped through the door. It was a picture of Joan the Wad, Queen of the Cornish piskies. On the back was written, "Dear both, had to get a temporary scribe to write this for me. Joan the Wad is a bringer of good luck. Couldn't think of anything more appropriate for us. Having a lovely time, but forgot me bucket and spade. Yours, Hugo."

I showed it to his mistress on her return.

'Hasn't lost his sense of humour. Hope the work is going well,' I said.

'We'll find out when he calls,' she replied.

***

Later that day my iPad sprang in to life: "I'm the urban spaceman baby; I've got speed, I've got everything I need. . ."

'It's Hugo!' I called as I hastily pressed Accept.

'Hugo, how are you?'

'Yer Ladyship, guv. I'm fine. Look at this,' he said. 'I've got me iPad on a moveable arm so I can lie in bed and talk to you, or push it around to show you me quarters.'

He pushed it a bit further away from him. He was lying in a comfortable memory foam bed, just like his one at home. He'd had the wall behind him decorated with some posters, including one captioned, "Bonzo's Cat and Dog Convalescent Home."

'What's with the convalescent home, Hugo?' we asked.

'It's brilliant,' he replied. 'Surprised you didn't see it when you dropped me off. There's a copy up in Reception. Missed it myself then. It's me old mate, Bonzo. Seems he's teamed up with Marmalade and opened up a convalescence and rest home on Ullswater, the other side from where we stayed. We must go and visit them.'

'We will, Hugo, I promise. How's the course going, and more to the point, how are you getting on? Any wobbles?'

'No, I've done alright so far. Take it one day at a time, as they say, but I'm cautiously optimistic. Miss you both a lot. Haven't got anybody to con for an extra treat . . . Only joking. Course is really interesting. We've been doing causes of addiction this week; looking at whether it's a chemical dependency on the substance itself or whether it's a behaviour associated with changes in the brain. They're suggesting that if you keep on engaging in overeating, your brain changes and eating triggers a pleasurable feeling of reward. Trouble is, that feeling of reward doesn't last, so you have to repeat the eating, and so on. Struggling a bit to get me head round it.'

'It sounds like you're doing very well, Hugo, we are really proud of you.'

'Thanks ever so much. Got to go now. It's time for me dinner.'

'Food any good?'

'Top notch, even had chicken biryani the other day. Better than being at home.'

'You're a rascal.'

'Just pulling your leg. It's me favourite Obesity Management for dogs. Call you tomorrow night about 10.00 o'clock, after me mindfulness session. Push the red button, guv.'

'Bye, Hugo!'

I ended the call.

***

This was the pattern for the next few weeks, until we were allowed down for an open day. Hugo was thrilled to see us, and couldn't wait to show us around and introduce us to his teachers.

'Ah, Hugo,' said his course leader. 'One of life's characters, isn't he? Wasn't sure at first that he was taking any of this seriously, but he's actually doing very well. Strange example of someone being the life and soul of the class whilst sitting at the front and studying diligently. He really is very hard-working, and I am sure he will do well. He has a lot of life experience that he can pass on. I suppose he really has had that experience, he's not making it up, is he?'

'I don't think so. I've met the Sitches in Soho, and Bonzo, and it all checks out. For all of his faults, he is a very honest dog.'

'Remarkable. We haven't told him, but if he carries on like this, he is going to come out top of his class.'

And, with that, his course leader moved on to speak to another set of owners. We went in search of Hugo, who had wandered off. We found him in his quarters, looking wistful.

'What's up, Hugo?'

'Not very good with crowds and, to tell the truth, I was thinking about Zoe. We've heard a lot recently from people who have been living with addicts. Telling us their side of the story; how their life was turned upside down. All the business of wanting to help but finding they couldn't do anything at all. How they felt rejected, and unloved, as they realised that the only thing the addict wanted was whatever they were addicted to. It was quite true. I only wanted food and I was nicest to those who would give it to me.

'One of the people who was talking to us was also saying how much harder it was because their addicted partner was always telling them that they were the one with all the faults. Thing was, it was the addict who had the faults, not the partner. My tutor said this was called "projection". I suddenly realised that I used to do that, blaming all around me for the faults that I had. Made me feel very ashamed. I wonder if it had anything to do with Zoe moving away?'

Hugo sat there looking very downcast.

His mistress looked at him. 'Hugo' she said, 'it doesn't do to sit there pitying yourself, you know. You have done terrifically well to get here, and your course leader says you are doing splendidly in your studies. Why don't you talk to Zoe? You know we've found her, and it will be another hurdle out of the way. Sort of a milestone on your road to success.'

Hugo looked thoughtful. 'I suppose you're right, but I'm still frightened of talking to her. You couldn't have a word with her first, could you? Sort of break the ice for me?'

'We'll do what we can, Hugo.'

We all sat there quietly for a bit, lost in our own thoughts. It had been quite a journey with Hugo, with lots of ups and downs. This was the first time that things had really looked remotely hopeful.

Hugo spoke again. 'When you come down at the end of the course, you couldn't bring Bonzo and Marmalade as well as Zoe, could you? I know they were my partners in crime, but we've all moved on now. Who'd have thought the two of them would end up in the Lake District? Quite a change for a pair of Londoners.'

'Of course we will.'

The bell rang for the end of our visit.

Hugo sat there looking disconsolate. 'One last thing. Any chance you could try and find the old soldier?'

'Of course, Hugo.'

'Wish I could come with you.'

'So do we, but you're nearly there, Hugo, and just think what an achievement this will be.'

'I know, guv, but I think 'Er Ladyship understands better. I want to be back with me family. You've no idea how important the two of you are to me. It's knowing you are there that keeps me going.'

'It's not long now, Hugo, and then you'll have your certificate and we will all be back together. Is your addiction really behind you?'

'For the moment, at least. Can't say more than that. Let's just say that I am still an addict, but in remission. Addiction is an illness that's lifelong, but I can get along at the moment without always thinking about food. I just have to stick to my daily rituals and remember the lessons I have learned. Being of assistance to others will be a help to me too. Make me feel good about myself. Anyway, time for you to go. I hate goodbyes. I'll call you tomorrow.'

'Bye, Hugo.'

And so, after the customary salutations, licks, strokes and cuddles, we went home.

Chapter 15

Graduation Day

The next few weeks were very busy. We contacted Fred and Doris, Zoe's owners, who were living in the Pennines in East Lancashire and told them about Hugo and Zoe and his graduation day. We arranged to meet up at their home, in a pretty little village with neat and tidy terraced houses, ornamental porches and immaculate flowered-filled front gardens – perfect territory for a manicured white poodle. We were shown into the front parlour.

'You will take some tea, won't you?'

'That would be lovely,' I replied.

'Is this your first visit to Rossendale?'

'Yes. I've some very good friends who come from the Ribble Valley, but I've not been to Rossendale before.'

'A talking Labrador? You're 'aving me on,' Fred said.

'Absolute truth.'

'How come Zoe doesn't talk, then?'

'She never learned, according to Hugo; but she does understand.'

Zoe jumped up and down, furiously nodding agreement.

'Ask her if she knew Hugo,' Doris said.

Zoe nodded.

'Ask her if she was at the St Martyn's School of Art as a life model.'

Again, Zoe nodded.

'Well, blow me down, and there was I thinking that "walkies" and "foodies" was all she understood!'

Zoe looked irritated and woofed quietly.

'Of course she can come down, but do you mind if we come? This is something we have to see.'

'We'll have to check with the principal, but I'm sure that will be OK.'

After a few more pleasantries, and lots of 'Well, I nevers', and Zoe bouncing around a room she was never normally let in, we made our excuses and left.

***

On return to London I set out to find the old soldier. My first thought was to ask the Sitch brothers, but they hadn't seen him for a long time. Nobody in St Anne's Court had heard of him, either, and the usual turnover of people meant that the group that had known him had all either moved on or died. I had one last thought. I wrote to the Royal Hospital in Chelsea and asked if, amongst their pensioners, was a former guardsman who had been living in a flat in Soho and who used to have a cat and, for a while, a dog called Hugo. About four weeks later I received a letter from a Sgt Major Jones, formerly of the Welsh Guards, and now an in-pensioner at the Royal Hospital. I went to see him.

The Royal Hospital was designed by Sir Christopher Wren and is one of the architectural gems of London. Hugo never mentioned it but, if he had ever been down there, he would wholeheartedly have approved of the building style. For most people it is best known as the place where the annual RHS Chelsea Flower Show is held. I met Sgt Major Jones in the coffee shop. He was a man in his early eighties, who still had the carriage of a guardsman, albeit now with a slight roll betokening arthritis in his hips. His face was careworn, but his eyes still sparkled. He was resplendent in his scarlet uniform and his shako hat. A row of medals betokened years of service to the Crown.

'Mr Jones, good to meet you. I believe we have a friend in common.'

'Thank you for your letter about Hugo. Surprised he's still alive! What's that rascal been up to now?'

I explained the story, amidst many, 'Well, well. Never would have believed it. He did turn out well.'

Eventually I got to the bit of Hugo having an end-of-course ceremony, and would he like to come down to Cornwall to see Hugo graduate.

'I would love to,' came the reply and so, after promising him that I would make sure he had transport to go down and a comfortable place to stay, I made to leave.

Mr Jones came with me to the gate.

'I'm really looking forward to seeing Hugo again,' he said. 'He was a lovely dog, but tormented by food. I'm glad he turned out well, but he did lead me a dreadful dance sometimes. I'm sure he never meant to, though, which was why I put up with him for so long.'

We sent out invitations to Bonzo and Marmalade and our friends, the Sitch brothers, who sadly had sold the brass lamp shop, bringing an end to thirteen generations of history.

The Sitches kindly offered to bring Mr Jones with them down to Cornwall.

After that we cleared up Hugo's corner, gave the area a good spring clean in honour of him coming home, and put the postcards he had sent us on the wall around his bed. Truth was, he had been away for far too long and we really missed him. I was sure my culinary skills had declined in the absence of him sitting under my feet commenting, 'More beef stock . . . should have used the rich one . . . go easy on the cardamom.' I missed the sight of him lolling on the couch in the study, waiting to ambush anybody going into the kitchen. On would go the Labrador-pleading-eyes as he appeared at the kitchen door, swearing blind that his last meal was over four hours ago rather than the fifteen minutes that had actually elapsed. It was all done in fun, of course, but he had a great knack of livening up the day. Not to have him around had been difficult, and it was going to be interesting to see if he had changed much whilst away on his therapy course.

About a week before graduation day the principal rang us. 'I have some good news for you,' he said, 'but you must keep it a secret. Hugo has come top of his class with a score of 97%. A remarkable achievement. He will, of course, get the prize for being Top Dog – richly deserved in my opinion, as he's worked really hard and has been very popular with all the staff and other dogs. Quite a sense of humour, though. Did you know he had started a book about picnic robbers and the "Great Black Hound of Hampstead Heath"?'

I changed the subject hurriedly.

***

Two days before Hugo's graduation there was a bang on the front door. We opened it to find Bonzo and Marmalade sitting there. How they had made it down from the Lake District was anyone's guess! And whilst both of them seemed to understand what we were saying, neither of them spoke. They took up residence on Hugo's downstairs bed, inspecting his postcards before settling in. They both came with us when we went for our walks on the Heath, and had that ease in their surroundings that showed they were on familiar territory.

***

The next day we all set off for Cornwall. Bonzo and Marmalade sat in the back, occasionally muttering to each other, but otherwise spent most of the time just sleeping. We reminisced about our previous trip down with Hugo and his lively interest in place names. Dogmersfield had been an obvious query of his, although it took a lot of explaining to him that it came from the Anglo Saxons. 'Who were the Anglo-Saxons, guv?' he'd asked, and we'd had a long diversion into early English history before we could get around to telling him that Dogmersfield meant "the land by the lake where the water lilies grow". Hugo had liked the poetry of that, but was disappointed by the lack of any canine connection.

Another query had been, 'Why is it called Polyphant? Is there an elephant connection?' – to which we had replied, 'No, Hugo, it's Cornish for "toads pool".' There had been a grumble from the back on that occasion. 'Doesn't anybody name anywhere after dogs?' he asked. I'd suggested the Isle of Dogs. Hugo was not amused. 'Never was a proper Isle of Dogs,' he'd said. 'Good idea, though. Perhaps we could have our own territory? They wrecked the Isle with all the glass and steel. I want something more uplifting.'

The best I could come up with was the story of Greyfriars Bobby in Edinburgh, and how he became so famous for his loyalty to his master's grave that the Lord Provost of Edinburgh himself paid for his dog licence. Hugo was very interested in this. He always liked stories of canine affection and devotion, but would often go into a long monologue, beating himself up over how useless a dog he had been. Changing the subject rarely helped, and it would take him a good night's sleep to recover his equilibrium.

That night we met up with Zoe's owners, Fred and Doris, at the pub we were staying in. The three animals settled down together in the corner of the garden whilst Her Ladyship went to get himself.

Hugo was terribly nervous when she found him. 'I can't do this,' he said, 'she's bound to be so cross with me.'

'Hugo, she's still in love with you. Of course she's sad about how you treated her, but she's always loved you. She's dying to see you again.'

When Hugo arrived, he stood at the open door still looking nervous. Bonzo and Marmalade held back, whilst Zoe rushed up to meet him, tail wagging furiously. Then the other two joined in, and there were joyous barks and meows, and much tail-wagging, sniffing and play-fighting. Eventually Bonzo and Marmalade came back to join us, leaving Hugo and Zoe on their own. We left them to it.

It was a lovely evening. Mr Jones told us a hilarious set of stories about Hugo as he sat in a corner seat, resplendent in his Chelsea pensioner's uniform. He was the centre of attraction in the pub that night – although most of his audience didn't quite get the significance of the black Labrador he was talking about.

Finally, it was time for bed. At first the two dogs feigned not to hear, but eventually they grudgingly appeared.

'Bit like separating a pair of lovesick teenagers,' remarked his mistress as she struggled to get Hugo to come over to have his lead put on. We took Hugo back to his quarters at the therapy school as he had to be up early the next morning. He was very quiet.

'Everything OK?' I asked.

'I've been a colossal idiot.'

'We all make mistakes.'

'Not as big as this.'

'What's the matter, Hugo?' his mistress asked.

'Oh, the whole addiction thing, and how it screws up your life and those you love.'

'You all seemed pretty happy tonight, how did it go with Zoe?'

'That's just the point, it went so well. Made me realise what I could have had if only I'd sorted myself out earlier.'

'But that's every addicts' thought. You could only sort yourself out when you did. You had to be ready for it,' I said.

'Took a long time, though, wish it hadn't.'

Hugo sighed and settled back, morosely, into his bed.

'Come on, cheer up. You're tired, it's been a long day, a lot has happened, and you need sleep. You'll feel much better in the morning.'

'Oh, I know that. Just having a wobble. It was wonderful seeing everyone again, but hard at the same time.'

'It looked as if it was alright with Zoe?'

'Like we'd never been apart. That's what made it tough. You're right, I'll be better in the morning. One last thing . . .'

'Yes?'

'I've been warned I might have to make a speech tomorrow. What do I say?'

'What does the speech have to be about?'

'Apparently, I have to say thank you on behalf of the class.'

'You'll do it splendidly. Do it from the heart. Make sure you say thank you to everybody, and particularly mention the people who get forgotten, like the ones who organised the event and did the catering. And, not to put too fine a point on it, knowing how messy you dogs can be, don't forget the unsung heroes who will have to clear up when it's all over.'

Hugo stared hard at me, made as if to say something, thought better of it and grumped off.

***

The next day was bright and sunny; one of those wonderful Cornish days when the sky is blue with puffy little white clouds driven by a stiffish breeze. Everything was light and clear, and the air smelt of the Atlantic with overtones of Scilly Isles' flowers. Hugo had his last classes to go to before the afternoon festivities, so the rest of us went for a morning walk along the coast path. After a while Marmalade found a spot on a dry-stone wall where she was out of the wind and could sunbathe. We left her to it; if she could get home from the north of Scotland there was little problem leaving her to doze for half an hour on a route we were going to have to retrace. We walked on, discussing how Hugo and Zoe might spend time together in the future.

'Is that the time?' Fred suddenly said.

'We must hurry back. We just have time for a quick lunch before we are due at the ceremony,' I replied.

We collected Marmalade, who was none too impressed at being disturbed having just got really warm and comfortable, and had a quick pub lunch before making our way across to the therapy school.

Everything was set up in a large marquee. At one end there was a raised dais with a table and chairs and a microphone on a stand. Immediately in front of the dais the ground was covered in blankets for the dogs, whilst further back were rows of folding seats for the guests. We found some seats at the front. Bonzo sprawled at our feet, whilst Zoe sat demurely with Fred and Doris. The Sitches and Mr Jones, resplendent once again in full dress uniform with medals and a tricorne hat, came to sit behind us, and Marmalade immediately made her way to greet them. Another visiting dog started to make trouble at the sight of a cat, only to be confronted by Marmalade with drawn claws and Bonzo suddenly breathing down his neck. He hurriedly withdrew and everybody settled down.

The buzz of conversation diminished on the arrival of the principal and staff, closely followed by the graduating dogs. Everybody took their places and the principal got up to speak.

'Ladies, gentlemen, dogs . . .' – and catching sight of Marmalade – 'and a remarkably brave cat.' Marmalade preened as every dog looked round and Bonzo edged closer to her as if to say to the other dogs, just try it on and see what happens. 'This is our fifth graduation ceremony and, I have to say, with each year the attitude and achievement of our students just keeps on getting better.'

A ripple of applause ran around the tent, together with a chorus of appreciative woofs.

'Today marks the end of a very important chapter in our student dogs' lives. All of them have had a very difficult start in life, and have confronted troublesome issues in themselves to even get here, let alone to successfully graduate. This year, for the first time, every dog on the course has graduated. That speaks volumes for the attitude of the dogs and the professionalism of my colleagues on the teaching staff. I am proud of all of you. It means a lot to get a therapist dog certificate.'

The principal turned to address the dogs. 'It shows commitment to work and commitment to developing yourselves. It means that you have not only managed to deal with your own addictions, but you have also shown the courage and commitment to take that experience and use it in the service of others. I know that not one of you is cured, for no addict ever is, but you have learnt how to live your life and control your addictive tendencies. For some of you, coming here has even meant giving up a highly successful business – picnic snaffling on Hampstead Heath, I believe – so a lot of sacrifice has been involved.'

My friend and I exchanged glances, hoping this theme would not be continued.

'It is up to you dogs to go out and look after others now. You can join the ranks of guide dogs, hearing dogs, helping dogs, and all the varied activities in which dogs have trained to help humans. We are very proud of you.

'Now is the time for you to receive your certificates and a special new collar for you to wear, embossed with the logo of our therapy school. Wear it with pride, remember what you are for, and remember that if ever you feel a bit wobbly, we are always here to help you.'

Much clapping and woofing followed.

'Without more ado, I would like each of you dogs, together with your owner, to come up and receive your certificate and collar.'

And so it started. A little alphabetic procession of dogs and owners shaking the principal's hand and collecting the treasured parchment that would allow the dog to practise as a therapist. We all cheered as Her Ladyship went up with Hugo, with Zoe leading the woofing. Eventually with Zebedee, a middle-aged rotund chocolate Labrador, the line came to an end and everybody returned to their seats.

The principal went back to the microphone.

'In any qualifying exam there is always one star amongst all the other stars who exceeds all expectations. This year's supernova, with the astonishing mark of 97% is . . . Hugo Labrador.'

We cheered furiously, Zoe ran round in circles barking her delight, and Bonzo and Marmalade jumped up and down in excitement. The other dogs graduating also woofed in support, showing that Hugo was clearly a popular choice.

The principal tapped the microphone to bring the proceedings to order and said, 'Hugo, would you like to say a few words?'

Hugo sat up to speak. The principal lowered the microphone for him, and a cameraman moved to get a better angle. Just audible over the PA system was a muttered, 'Darn black Labradors, they're impossible to photograph.'

Hugo coughed nervously and cleared his throat. 'Ladies and gentlemen, my friends,' – as he looked at Bonzo, Zoe and

Marmalade – 'Yer Ladyship, guv. I feel ever so humbled to be here and to receive this prize. If it 'adn't been for all the help I've had over the years I would never have got here today. Some of you had to see me get to rock-bottom before I got enough motivation to sort meself out. That is so often the way with addicts. To all of you I say a heartfelt thank you, and an enormous "I'm sorry" for all the trouble I've caused.'

The audience went very quiet as everybody reflected on their own experience with addicts, and as an addict.

Hugo continued, saying, 'All of us dogs owe a tremendous amount to the staff of the therapy school for helping us to achieve our certificates. On behalf of the other dogs I would like to thank all the other folk who have tried to help us in the past. It cannot have been easy. There are some who I would like to thank in particular. To name them all would mean everybody going hungry for another hour or two,' – a groan came from the audience – 'but I must single out a few. Reggie my pit bull friend at the dogs home, who sent me down here; my friends the Sitches, who welcomed me into their shop so I could have a warm up by their hearth; the old soldier, Mr Jones, who I am delighted to see in the audience; and finally 'Er Ladyship for her love, devotion and belief in me, and the guv for being me scribe and part-time companion.'

'Now, I've been told the art of public speaking is to keep things short and not go snowflake on you like they do at the Oscars. I'm also told the caterers have laid on a wonderful spread,' – cheers and a collection of woofs went up from the audience – 'of which I shall not, of course, partake,' – a chorus of 'Oh, really?' came from the assembled dogs – 'as I shall stick to my diet of Evian water and Obesity Management for dogs.' At this point Bonzo put his paws over his ears and

Marmalade almost split her sides with laughter. 'Although I can highly recommend the mini hamburgers – Waitrose party food, if I'm not mistaken! And, please, may I ask you to spare a thought for the kindly souls who will have to clear up after a party of celebratory dogs. Don't make their task too hard!' he added.

He became more serious. 'It's very difficult as an addict because you can only convince people you have changed by your actions. I know I shall always be at risk of succumbing to a passing cote du boeuf or chicken biryani or,' – he looked pointedly in my direction – 'a blue lobster; but for the moment I am remission, and I intend to do what I can to help others and trust that I don't succumb any more to the likes of chocolate fondant cake.' A groan came from somewhere in the audience. 'Thank you all for helping me, and for helping us, and thank you for this wonderful prize.'

Hugo shuffled round to face the principal, who was holding a large flat box in front of him.

'What is the prize may I ask?' Hugo asked.

The principal took the microphone again. 'Hugo Labrador, in recognition of your sterling efforts and coming out as Top Dog in the Class of 2017, we award you this engraved silver and leather collar to wear on high days and holidays, and to be hung by your bed with – so we hear – the postcards you sent home.'

Hugo woofed graciously, and then the PA picked up, for all to hear, Hugo's sotto voce: 'I could have sworn it was a Belgian apple pie in that box.'

Chapter 16

Postscript

Hugo came back with us that night and we had a small celebratory dinner with Fred and Doris, the Sitches, Mr Jones, Zoe, Bonzo and Marmalade. There was much more reminiscing. Marmalade was the life and soul of the party and had the dogs in hysterics. Hugo translated some of the stories, but we had the strong impression that the more outrageous escapades were being censored. Eventually we went to bed.

***

The next morning, we sat down with Fred and Doris over breakfast. We had important matters to discuss. Hugo and Zoe obviously wanted to spend as much time together as they could, but they both now had commitments. We settled on the obvious: Hugo and Zoe would take it in turns to stay with each other for a while, every month or so. Hugo was keen to get on with his therapy work, and Zoe had her own commitments in East Lancashire, but at least this way they got to maximise their time together.

Later on that day we said our goodbyes. Bonzo and Marmalade headed back up to the Lake District, and Hugo and Zoe promised to visit when they were next up north. Fred and Doris, who were a little bemused by events, promised to look after Hugo when he came to stay. The Sitches were their usual delightful selves, and promised the three dogs and Marmalade that there would always be a welcome for them whenever they were in London. Mr Jones invited Hugo to come and see him in the Royal Hospital whenever he was passing, an invitation that Hugo gratefully accepted. Finally, Hugo, Her Ladyship and I paid our bills and went home. It all went very quiet.

'It will be good to get back, guv.'

'Certainly will.'

'Any changes?'

'Well, your bed area is tidier, so you'll have space on your bit of wall for your certificates and collar, and all the dog food has been lifted out of your way in the utility room.'

'Sorry about me joint tablets.'

Hugo had alluded to an episode just before we took him down to therapy school, when he had eaten an entire jar of chondroitin and glucosamine tablets.

'I still don't know how you did that. The lid was on tight.'

'Not sure myself. Must be developing opposable thumbs.'

'You're a rogue. What about all the tooth marks in the plastic. They were from the inside out.'

'Just trying to make sure I didn't miss a tablet.'

'You must have had jolly supple joints after that!'

'S'pose so. I was too busy studying to notice. We anywhere near Dogmersfield yet? I like that name.'

'In about an hour, Hugo, want to stop?'

'Not really, just like the name. Night-night.'

And with that he twirled around in his bed at the back of the car and went to sleep.

***

The next day I took Hugo down to town to register his new qualification. The Society of Therapist Dogs had its headquarters in Meard Street in Soho, just around the corner from so many of his adventures.

'It seems strange being back here, guv, all me old haunts and me new future right in the middle of it.'

We watched as his name was carefully entered into a beautifully bound book listing all the therapist dogs to date. His entry was at the top of a new page: "Admitted, 26 August 2017, Hugo Labrador, Graduated Abbey School for Therapist Dogs."

'A proud moment, Hugo.'

'Certainly is, guv. Quite a journey for a Bermondsey Labrador.'

We walked round the corner and had a cup of tea with the Sitches in Pret A Manger.

'We always loved you, young Hugo,' they said. 'Bit of a lad, but a heart of gold. Glad things have worked out well for you.'

Hugo looked thoughtful. 'I do know it's a chronic illness I have,' he said, 'and I shall never be free of it, but at least I know how to manage it. Time to pass on some of my skills now.'

Laurence said, 'I have something for you.' And he handed Hugo a small thin parcel about the size of an iPhone. We opened it up. Inside was a brass plaque with "Hugo Labrador, Registered Therapist Dog" engraved upon it.

'There you are, Hugo,' I said, 'your own shingle to hang up. We'll put it outside the front door and you can join a really select list of Hampstead analysts and therapists. Now you have to get clients.'

'Can I start with you, guv?'

'No. That bird has flown. You did me a lot of good, though. You gave me an entirely different book to the one I was going to write.'

When we got home I fixed Hugo's brass plaque just beside the front door, about three feet off the ground.

'You'll need to move the bell as well.'

'I thought you were having human patients?'

'What did you put the plaque down there for then?'

'Thought you might want to see it. Anyway, at this height both dogs and humans can see it.'

'Very kind of you. Can I use the couch in the study for me therapy sessions?'

'You'll have to ask 'Er Ladyship.'

***

Quite a few weeks later Hugo and I got up very early and drove to Aldeburgh. He had always wanted to see the sun rise over the sea. We had both been busy, me with my book and Hugo with his first clients and a long visit up to stay with Zoe. The schools were back and the beaches were empty once more. We parked near the fishermen's huts. The fishermen were moving around in the near darkness, getting their boats ready to go out on the morning tide. We sat down on the shingle.

'You alright, Hugo?'

'Never better. It's like coming out of a long tunnel. I've got Zoe back in me life, a proper job, and a loving pack around me. Never thought it would happen. I've got everything to live for.'

'How is it working out with Zoe?'

'As if we had never been apart. Better than ever it was before. Can be difficult, though.'

'Yes?'

'I miss her dreadfully when we're not together. But we have responsibilities. She's got her pack to look after and I've got mine. Us dogs do loyalty, but that doesn't stop us wishing . . .' He trailed off.

'Can we help?'

'Not really, guv. You and 'Er Ladyship have been marvellous. Facetime helps, as well as the lifts to the station. Who knows, maybe one day I'll have a private jet.'

'You're a rascal.'

Can't help it.'

Slowly the horizon lightened with the rays of the still-hidden sun striking the high clouds, suffusing the sky red and gold.

'You're a lucky dog, you know.'

'Oh, I know. This happens to very few addicts. Could still fall apart for me, but I've learnt a lot and I have some very useful skills to help me. You sure you're alright, guv?'

'In great shape, Hugo. You and Her Ladyship have been wonderful. I've finished one book, and I've already started the one I originally intended to write.'

'Are you going to stay?'

'What, as in stay around?'

'Yes.'

'I don't know. I would like to, but it's important not to overstay one's welcome. What's the phrase? "Guests and fish go off after three days." Still, I think we've got a few more adventures left in us, don't you?' I've also got a few health issues to sort out.'

'I think 'Er Ladyship would like it.'

'Kind of you to say so. We'll see what happens. Perhaps we can persuade her to come with us on some of our walks and travels.'

'That would be nice. Guv?'

'Yes, Hugo.'

'Did you ever read any Douglas Adams?'

'Yes, why?'

I've got a quote of his that pretty much sums up me life.'

'Go on . . .'

'"I may not have gone where I intended to go, but I think I ended up where I needed to be".'

'I think that sums up your life perfectly, Hugo.'

'Guv?'

'Hugo?'

'Can we watch the sun set over the sea?'

'Not from here. We'll have to go to the west coast for that. It would be best from the Western Isles.'

'Maybe that's our next adventure. Why don't we put it on the planner? Perhaps we could start the next book that way?'

'Done. Now, you've been pestering me about those lobsters. Isn't it time to go?'

'Not just yet, I want to watch the boats go out.'

So we sat on the beach together, and Hugo cuddled into me and watched the sunrise as the fishing boats slipped quietly into the water on the rising tide.

THE END